Cameron's Commitment

BY THE SAME AUTHOR:

Cameron's Commitment

Philip McCutchan

St. Martin's Press   New York

CAMERON'S COMMITMENT. Copyright © 1989 by Philip McCutchan. All rights
reserved. Printed in the United States of America. No part of this book may be
used or reproduced in any manner whatsoever without written permission
except in the case of brief quotations embodied in critical articles or reviews.
For information, address St. Martin's Press, 175 Fifth Avenue, New York, N.Y.
10010.

Library of Congress Cataloging-in-Publication Data

McCutchan, Philip.
        Cameron's commitment.

        1. World War, 1939-1945—Fiction.   2. Great Britain—
History, Naval—20th century—Fiction.   I. Title.
PR6063.A167C337   1989   823'.914   88-30172
ISBN 0-312-02532-7

First published in Great Britain by George Weidenfeld & Nicolson Ltd.
First U.S. Edition
10 9 8 7 6 5 4 3 2 1

Cameron's Commitment

1

THE UNBERTHING parties, a motley crowd of dockyard mateys, stood by on the South Railway Jetty where in peacetime the battleship that wore the flag of Commander-in-Chief Home Fleet had customarily berthed when in Portsmouth harbour. Now the great battleships and battle-cruisers were dispersed from the southern ports to lie in the safer waters of Scapa Flow, or the Forth, or the Clyde, exiles from their home bases, sea-worn, lying at anchor or at buoys, leaving the convenience of the South Railway Jetty to the smaller units of the fleet. From the navigating bridge of HMS *Castile*, a C Class light cruiser with much of her main armament of six-inch guns stripped away and replaced by anti-aircraft guns and close-range weapons, Cameron looked through a murky drizzle, down at the clustered, wettened dockyard mateys, across towards Nelson's flagship *Victory* in her dry dock, and then, closer at hand, at the signal tower that loomed behind the jetty. The routine reports were already in: First Lieutenant to report the ship's company aboard and correct, the divisions standing by fore and aft to let go the wires and ropes, and the ship in all respects ready for sea; engineer officer to report his engines awaiting the telegraphed order from the bridge to proceed.

Cameron spoke to his navigating officer.

'All set, Pilot?'

'All set, sir.'

'Yeoman?'

'Sir?' Yeoman of Signals Robbins, a fleet reservist – a recalled pensioner – like most of the *Castile*'s senior lower deck ratings, came forward, signal pad and pencil at the ready.

'Request permission to proceed in execution of orders.'

'Aye, aye, sir.' Robbins turned away, nodded at his leading signalman. The message was passed to the King's Harbour Master and almost on its heels the reply came back and Robbins reported. 'Permission to proceed, sir.'

'Thank you, Yeoman.' Cameron moved to the Tannoy, switched on and passed the unberthing orders fore and aft. 'Let go head and stern wires, let go spring.' He waited while this was done and the reports had come from the fo'c'sle and quarterdeck. With the ship now held only on the backspring, a heavy wire leading from aft in the ship to a set of bollards for'ard on the jetty, and her bows pointing for the harbour exit into the waters of Spithead, Cameron passed the orders for the engines to move slow astern with the wheel amidships. As the sternway reacted against the hold of the backspring, *Castile*'s bows swung off to starboard, aiming her course clear of the jetty.

'Let go backspring.'

'Let go backspring, sir.' That was the quarterdeck divisional officer, who was also *Castile*'s gunnery officer – Peter Blake, an RNVR lieutenant. Cameron lifted a hand in acknowledgement and glanced at the navigator.

'All right, Pilot. Take her away. Engines half ahead.'

The telegraph handles were pulled over below in the wheelhouse to be repeated in the engine-room. Lieutenant(E) Rogers, a regular RN officer, watched as his chief engine-room artificer operated the tell-tale that would confirm to the bridge that the order had been received and obeyed. The din in the engine-room grew as the shafts revolved faster. Ratings moved about with long-necked oilcans, checking bearings, dabbing oil here and there. Up

6

in the wheelhouse, Chief Petty Officer Barker, chief quartermaster, on the wheel when entering or leaving harbour and when in action, moved the wheel in response to orders from the navigator, heading the old cruiser for the narrows of the harbour entrance. He lit a fag and blew smoke thoughtfully: there was something weird about this departure. As usual in wartime, the ship's company was in the dark as to the orders, but anyone could make guesses and many guesses had been made . . . and there was one thing for sure in Barker's mind and that was that there was something personal about the *Castile* for the skipper. He knew that because Cameron had told him so when the ship had been recommissioned with a new ship's company, after a minor refit just to make her seaworthy after a Jerry shell had ripped through the seamens' messdeck some weeks earlier and left a nasty hole and a lot of blood. There was also something special for CPO Barker himself: he'd done no less than two full commissions in the old *Castile* in peacetime, back in the twenties and again, the second one, in the thirties – in fact she'd been his last ship before going out on pension to a totally different life working as a postman. The *Castile*'s wheelhouse was like home in a sense – he'd been Chief QM on that second commission, just like now.

The funny thing was, something similar applied to almost all the RFR men aboard. Some of them had been with CPO Barker: they were personal friends. Someone at the Admiralty, or more likely in the Drafting Master-at-Arms' office in Pompey barracks, had a warped sense of humour. All old crocks together, in an old crock of a ship.

HMS *Castile* moved on, past the Southern Railway's harbour station with the mudlarks grubbing for thrown pennies in the creek behind, past the Ryde paddle-steamer waiting at the pier, past the *Vernon* torpedo school, past the Camber, past a couple of pubs well known to most of her company, the Still and West and the Coal Exchange, past, on the other side, Fort Blockhouse with a number of submarines lying in trots like trawlers, alongside each other. Then out and away past the Round Tower, Clarence Pier and Southsea Castle, the Naval War Memorial and the Queens Hotel in the background, to make the turn to starboard as soon as the transits came on in the navigator's azimuth circle.

It was all very peaceful, as Able Seaman Bottomley, one of the relief quartermasters, remarked. 'Wouldn't think there was a war on, eh, Chief?'

'That's Pompey for you, Stripey. All lovely and quiet until the bloody *Luftwaffe* comes over.'

'No *Luftwaffe* now.'

'There will be.' Barker stubbed out his fag in a tin beside the wheel housing. 'There's something funny up. Reduced complement, just for one thing. *And* the skipper. RNVR . . . you don't often get *any* RNVR commanding a light cruiser, let alone a two-and-a-half striper.' A four-ring captain RN would be the norm. 'Mind, Cameron's got a good record. You don't get a DSC for sod all.'

ii

The CW Lists were published daily in wartime whether or not you were on leave, as Cameron was when his appointment came through from the office of the Naval Assistant to the Second Sea Lord – NA2SL in navalese – in Queen Anne's Mansions, London. It came just as Cameron and his parents were finishing breakfast at home in Aberdeen, and it came in the form of a telegram addressed Lieutenant-Commander D.P.Cameron RNVR and it read simply: *You are appointed Castile in command stop you are required to attend NA2SL 1100 Friday 4 March.*

'Tomorrow,' Cameron senior said.

'A pierhead jump!'

'Yes . . . .' Captain Cameron, a master mariner now retired from seagoing and running his own trawler fleet out of Aberdeen, seemed in something of a reverie. 'You did say *Castile*?'

8

'I did indeed.' Cameron passed the telegram over. His father had served in the *Castile* and now proceeded to reminisce.

'Tail end of the last war. One of the early ones of her class, commissioned in 1917 . . . not far off, what, twenty-seven years ago! I didn't think she was still afloat to be honest.' Captain Cameron's thoughts were right back in the past. He'd been a lieutenant RNR then, and the *Castile* had been his last ship as such. He went on, 'You know the story, of course. We fell in with a German light cruiser squadron. We were messed about a bit . . . we beat off the Jerries in the end and we got back into Scapa . . . later, we watched the German High Seas Fleet coming in to surrender. I saw that from the old *Castile*'s bridge . . . .'

He went on to relive the past: Cameron had heard it all before. His father had lost a good shipmate, a good friend, in the action against the German squadron – the doctor. He'd gone onto the fo'c'sle where one of a gun's-crew was lying wounded and helpless, the only one of that gun's-crew to survive. A shell had come over just as the doctor had got there, and he took it. He'd been a grand fellow, Captain Cameron said – sailed with him before the Great War, ship's surgeon in the Pacific Steam Navigation Company's liner *Ortega*. 'Saved my life once,' Captain Cameron went on, a distant look in his eyes. 'A nasty spot of bother ashore in Rio – we were younger then! Too much to drink, and the dago knives were out.' He paused. 'Well – you know all that. I'm getting garrulous in my old age!'

'It's all right, Dad. It bears repeating!' Cameron grinned.

'Yes, well.' His father passed a hand across his eyes. 'It's a rum world, Donald. I'd never have thought that one day my son would find himself in command of the old *Castile*.' Abruptly, he pushed his chair back and got to his feet. 'You're honoured.' He pre-empted the sentiments yet to be expressed by Chief Petty Officer Barker. 'A four-ring captain's command! Yes, you're honoured. Be worthy of it – right? She's a good ship. Look after her for me. Treat her well. Bring her through – whatever's to come.'

He left the room.

It had been a longish speech for a normally taciturn man and there had been emotion, well controlled. Cameron glanced at his mother, and smiled. They both knew ships, and the sea, and the men who sailed the ships on that sea. There was any amount of sentimentality, any amount of nostalgia, and the younger Cameron understood his father well. For himself, there would be something extra about the *Castile*, some special quality, a particular retrospective knowledge, not exactly a memory of course, but scenes he would be able to visualize of the old light cruiser in action with his father in that earlier conflict. And now, two weeks later, as he took the *Castile* out of Portsmouth harbour in execution of previous orders, he was one of a very few people who knew that it was to be for the last time. Very far from what his father had been hopeful of . . . .

His mind went back, as his navigating officer began to line up his bearings on the spire of St Jude's Church in Southsea, to his visit to the office of NA2SL.

iii

The officer who interviewed him was a Captain RN, tall, grey-haired, concise. There was no name on the door of his office, and Cameron never did learn his identity. He started off by asking Cameron if he didn't find it strange that he was being appointed in command of a light cruiser.

'I do, sir. Destroyers –'

'Yes, I'm naturally aware you've done most of your time in destroyers. Light cruisers are little more than large destroyers really, although of course their role is different in some ways. That's to say, they're not employed exclusively on convoy escort duty. And the *Castile*'s going on no convoy. But the main reason for your appointment is yourself, Cameron.'

'I see, sir . . . .'

The Captain smiled briefly. 'I doubt if you do. I'll tell

you: you've been employed on special missions, special operations. Not once, but four times. The extrication of a Greek freedom fighter from Crete. The operation against the German base in that Norwegian fjord. The cutting-out of the *Kaiserhof* from Cadiz. The Brest raid. In all cases, you did well.'

'Thank you, sir.'

'So to some extent you're a marked man. You're known in high places, very high places indeed. The operation you'll be going on . . . it's of vital importance to our strategy. It's a scheme of Mr Churchill's and he's taking a personal interest. He's very insistent, and he's right – which he hasn't always been, between you and me. Having said that, I can't add anything more – I'm concerned with officer appointments, not operations strictly. You'll be going on elsewhere for a briefing. But there's just one thing I can tell you, Cameron, and it's this: Mr Churchill's got an odd bee in his bonnet concerning the *Castile*. I happened to dig out the fact that your father served in the ship on her first commission and I passed it on. That gave the PM ideas. He's let it be known that he wishes as many of her new ship's company as possible to come from the *Castile*'s previous commissions, and that's being attended to via the Drafting Commander at RNB Portsmouth – she was always a Portsmouth Port Division ship. And via me. For instance, your First Lieutenant's to be a fellow named John Brown, a first-rate officer ex lower deck, a former upper yardman who came up to mate and sub-lieutenant, thence lieutenant. He served in *Castile* as a leading seaman on the China station in the mid thirties. Your gunner, Mr Marty, was a gunner's mate in *Castile* in the East Indies. Your engineer officer, Rogers, sailed in her as a sub-lieutenant(E) just before the war, in the Mediterranean. All the rest of your officers will be RNR and RNVR. For the lower deck, you'll have the usual mixture – some active service RN, some HO, some fleet reservists. The latter will predominate, thanks to Mr Churchill's wishes. Any questions?'

11

'Just one, sir. Why does Mr Churchill want so many men from previous commissions?'

The Captain shrugged. '*Esprit de corps! Esprit de Castile*, in fact. As I said, this mission's regarded as of extreme importance. Mr Churchill believes that if so many of her company come from shared experiences, there'll be an extra effort towards total success. They won't want to let the old ship down. I've no doubt you've come to know the way seamen look at things – they're a very loyal lot, and the *Castile* was always a happy ship.'

For loyal read sentimental – that word again – was Cameron's thought as he left Queen Anne's Mansions and walked across Green Park towards the Admiralty building with its great brick bunker built onto its side by Horse Guards Parade. But it was true that all seamen had a special fondness for a ship with a happy reputation. Some ships got off to a bad start, and spent their lives as unhappy ships where each man was at the next man's throat and there was a bad feeling between wardroom and lower deck; others were the opposite. Among the happy ships was the battleship *Rodney*. The battle-cruiser *Repulse*, now at the bottom of the South China Sea with the *Prince of Wales*, had been another. Ships were very human and undoubtedly, to a seaman, had souls.

One hour later, leaving the Admiralty's Operations Division, Cameron was in possession of all the facts. He didn't like the implications at all. There was no denying the importance of what he had to achieve but he wondered if Mr Churchill had got it right when he'd insisted on the previous-commissions element. Cameron's own feeling was that he very likely had not, but it remained to be seen. Cameron's view was that no-one wanted to see a happy ship die, much less so when they'd spent good years aboard her in a distant past. And the *Castile* was certainly booked to die, and a lot of men would die with her. Such was war.

Cameron looked at his watch: time for lunch, if wartime London could provide it. He walked along the Mall, up the

12

Duke of York's Steps, past the Athenaeum. It was a windy March day, with streaky white cloud scudding along. He made his way to the Piccadilly Hotel and after a gin-and-bitters bought himself lunch. Then he used the telephone and tried a few numbers on spec. He was to take up his new command the following day at 1000 hours: he would spend the night in London, but hoped it wouldn't have to be on his own. The third number brought success: a girl named Jean, an ATS working at the War Office who had a couple of days' leave and was at a loose end. As well as leave she had a small flat in Oakley Street, Chelsea. And she was delighted to be asked.

Next morning Cameron just about caught his train from Waterloo for Portsmouth Harbour station, where on arrival he looked with a sense of at least temporary possession at the two funnels and masts of HMS *Castile* at the South Railway Jetty a stone's throw from the station.

2

THE SHIP WAS long and slender, not too much beam, displacement 4200 tons, graceful as warships of her generation had always been, her lines not marred by her camouflage paint. Mr Marty, gunner RN, joining a couple of days before Cameron, had got out of the taxi that had brought him from the harbour station through the main gate of the dockyard, and had stood there just looking at her while a party of ratings had carried his gear aboard.

His old ship: he'd not seen her since he'd left her as a leading seaman nearly twenty years before, when she'd returned from Singapore to pay off here in Pompey, with her paying-off pennant floating away astern over the spotless quarterdeck. There had been a lot of brasswork in those days – brass bollards for instance, now replaced during subsequent refits by modern Staybrite steel like the new cruisers, and even that painted over after war had broken out. Not the same thing at all; yet Mr Marty was glad to rejoin, like a man going back to an old love who had changed a little in the passing years but was still basically the same. And now he was rejoining as a gunner, a warrant officer with a single thin gold stripe on his cuff, and an officer's badge resplendent on his cap. Even apart from the ship herself, Mr Marty was glad to be going back to sea. After recall in 1939 he'd been appointed to the training service and his last job had been at HMS *Royal Arthur* at

Skegness, formerly a Butlin's holiday campsite, where the new entries of Hostilities-Only ratings were given their first experience of naval life. Of course, it hadn't been entirely a bad patch; the youngsters – in fact many of them were more than that – had mostly been keen to learn and anxious to have a crack at Hitler. Some had been volunteers, some conscripts, but after a few weeks you wouldn't have known the difference. It had been heartening to a middle-aged gunner who until then had tended to think that the new generation would never have the guts for war that the older men had had back in 1914. But Mr Marty's heart was at sea.

Naturally, his wife Bess hadn't been pleased when the draft had come through; they'd got a nice couple of rooms with a seaside landlady and Bess had been happy to have a husband home most nights, but things couldn't last for ever and as a naval wife of many years' standing she understood this.

'Besides,' he'd said when his appointment had come through, 'it's the old *Castile*. Remember, eh?'

'Of course I do, Arthur.' Bess Marty, like her husband, was as round as a bun, as comfortable as a ball of knitting wool. She hadn't always been; once, she'd been slim – not tall, but a nice figure, and mens' eyes had followed her often enough. In the twenties she'd lived in Portsmouth, her father being a dockyard worker, and she'd gone aboard the *Castile* when the ship had had an Open Day after the 1926 fleet review and the eyes of Leading Seaman Marty had followed her to very good effect. He'd manoeuvred her behind a six-inch gun-shield to show her the breech mechanism or something, neatly cutting her out from her mum who'd gone chasing around like a bewildered hen or, as Leading Seaman Marty had put it, a blue-arsed fly. The advent of a petty officer had prevented any immediate developments but they'd made a date for Arthur's next night ashore and he'd taken her to the Hippodrome after a fish-and-chip supper in Commercial Road. It had been a swift romance, love at first sight and all that, and despite

15

opposition from mum and dad, they'd got married at Kingston church in Portsmouth; and within a few days *Castile* had been under orders to join the East Indies Squadron in Singapore. Arthur Marty had sailed away and Bess hadn't set eyes on him for the next two years.

Yes, she remembered the old *Castile* all right. She remembered the bursting feeling in her heart as she'd waved towards the outward-bound light cruiser from a sea wall near the Round Tower at the harbour entrance, hoping to see Arthur fallen in with his division for leaving harbour. That two years had gone by like lead. Since then there had been other foreign commissions. When this time the moment came to say goodbye at Skegness railway station, she was to some extent hardened to partings but there was a difference because there was a war on now.

'Take care, Arthur.'

'Course I will, love.'

'Keep away from them Germans.'

He laughed. 'Do me best, eh.'

There were tears in her eyes. 'Come back safe, Arthur.'

'Yes,' he said, 'I will.'

Standing alongside the *Castile*, thinking of many things past, Mr Marty recalled those last words as a promise. Yes, he would come back safe. If he didn't, it would go very hard with Bess. God must surely understand that. Yet, when he climbed the gangway and set foot on the *Castile*'s quarterdeck, and saluted, he found a doubt at the back of his mind. There was something funny in the air, almost a premonition, a curious feeling of finality, he couldn't have said why . . . .

An RNVR sub-lieutenant, Officer of the Watch with dangling sword belt empty of any sword in indication of his current duty, returned Marty's salute.

'Joining the ship, sir,' Mr Marty said, all very formal on joining, the one and only time he would be addressing any sub-lieutenant as sir. 'Name o' Marty, gunner RN.'

'Welcome aboard, Mr Marty.' They shook hands.

16

'Been changes,' Mr Marty said, looking around proprietorially.

'You've been in the ship before, have you?'

'Oh yes,' Mr Marty said. 'Old *Castile* hand, that's me.'

'That's funny. You're not the only one. Number One and the Chief – they've both served in earlier commissions. Lieutenant Brown and Lieutenant(E) Rogers.'

'Don't know 'em,' Mr Marty said. 'After my time, I reckon.'

'There's others on the lower deck. Chief QM, buffer, yeoman of signals, chief stoker . . . and your own chief gunner's mate come to that.'

'Name of?'

'Shine. Chief PO Shine – '

'Well, I'll be buggered,' Mr Marty said, surprised but pleased. 'Bullshit Shine . . . loading number with me on A gun! Unless there's some coincidence of name.'

There was no coincidence. It was Bullshit Shine right enough, as large as life and twice as noisy. He'd always had a loud voice for a small bloke like a sparrow, Marty remembered, but he was good at his job, or had been. Later that day Mr Marty discovered more ex-*Castiles* than the RNVR sub had catalogued and, nice though it was to exchange reminiscences of different commissions all over the Empire, Mr Marty's misgivings grew. It was almost like a family gathering over a relative about to die.

ii

Changes there certainly had been: Marty knew and was grieved that the six-inch guns had been taken out, all of them except for the two mountings on the fo'c'sle, the rest being ack-ack.

'Means one thing, sir,' Chief PO Shine said.

'Look, for a start, you don't need to call me sir except when we're being formal. Which we're not, now. All right?'

'All right, Arthur.' Bullshit Shine sounded pleased.

'Right! Well, What does it mean?'

'Means no rearguard action to come. No turning tail. We head right for it.'

'Head right for what?'

Shine shrugged. 'Ask me another.'

'No buzzes?'

'Only the usual load of crap.'

'Such as?'

'Oh, we're going to act as ack-ack guard to escort Winnie up the Rhine. Ditto to meet Eisenhower, coming over from the States to start the second front they've been yacking about for the last – '

'Yes. Time they got on with that, relieve the pressure on the Russian front.'

'That's another buzz, Arthur. We're going through the bleeding Dardanelles . . . taking Monty to advise Timoshenko how to knock the Jerries for six. Talking of Timoshenko . . . did you know he was Irish?'

'Get away with you!'

'It's true. Tim O'Shenko, old Irish family, migrated to – '

Marty dug him in the ribs. 'Still the same old Bullshit. Put a sock in it. I want a good creep around the armament. No time like the present. Who's the gunnery officer?'

'Not aboard yet. I hear he's an RNVR two-striper.'

Mr Marty said, 'We'll lick him into shape, eh?' He followed his new chief gunner's mate around the upper deck, making mental notes. Radar aerials loomed at the foremast head. Like all ships since the outbreak of war the old light cruiser had been fitted with paravanes that would be streamed on either bow at sea so as to cut the moorings of mines and let them loose to be deflected by the bow wave and then blown up by rifle fire. Likewise de-gaussing gear, heavy electric cable that ran right around the ship as an antidote to the new-fangled magnetic mines. Kept the ship's magnetic field from straying outboard or something, Mr Marty reckoned, though he didn't know a lot about it. Job of the torpedomen, was that. But now he'd have to learn

18

about it since the *Castile* no longer carried a torpedo-gunner
– the eight tubes had been taken out at a refit back in 1941,
Shine said informatively.

'I know. I keep up to date when I've got the time. There
was something in AFOs – alterations and additions. When
do we leave for sea, d'you know?'

Shine shook his head. 'No. Won't be for a week or so,
though, I reckon. Ship's far from fully stored yet and
anyway we're not up to complement.'

'We're not going to be, for my money, old lad.'

Shine lifted an eyebrow. 'How's that, then?'

'RNVR two-and-a-half in command, that's how. Full
complement would demand four rings.'

'Well, that's a thought.' Shine paused, gaze running
automatically over his fo'c'sle-mounted guns. 'What do *you*
reckon we're booked for, eh?'

'No idea, none at all. Care-and-maintenance up beyond
Whaley, swinging round a bleeding buoy, for all I know!'

'That'd be the day,' Shine said grimly. He'd done his
share of sea-time since 1939, in other cruisers mostly, and
he could do with a spell in Pompey, which was where his
home was – or had been until he'd evacuated the wife to
Rowlands Castle just the other side of Portsdown Hill,
handy when you got night leave, just a bus ride but a sight
safer for the family than Pompey in the blitz. The Jerries
didn't bother to bomb the villages, but often at night you
could see the fires over the town and dockyard, or anyway
the loom of them lighting the sky like a preview of hell.
Bullshit Shine had been on a fourteen-day leave the night
the Nazis dropped a land mine on the petty officers' mess in
the barracks back in early 1941, and he would never forget
what he saw the next day when he walked along Queen
Street. He'd lost some old mates that night.

'Tell you what,' Mr Marty said suddenly, lifting his cap
and scratching his forehead.

'Yes?'

'What about a reunion ashore? As many old *Castiles* as
aren't watch aboard.'

'Count me in, though I won't make it late. Time's precious.'

'Thinking of home?'

'That's right.'

'I s'pose you got married, like all daft matlows . . . .'

iii

They met the following evening, though 'met' was scarcely the word: they went ashore in a bunch, Mr Marty, Chief PO Shine, Chief Stoker Rump, Chief PO Barker, Yeoman of Signals Robbins, and Chief PO Froggett, chief bosun's mate, senior man of the lower deck. They drank Brickwood's bitter in a pub in Queen Street, spiritual home of all roistering Pompey division ratings, and they talked of times past, of those old commissions in the piping days of peace, showing the flag around the Empire, carrying out combined manoeuvres with the Home and Mediterranean Fleets, riding in rickshaws in Hong Kong and Singapore, lying typhoon racked in the Bay of Bengal or fighting through the westerlies on passage from Fremantle in Western Australia to the Cape of Good Hope and a spell ashore in Simonstown or Cape Town. Other times here in Pompey or swinging at anchor off Invergordon in Scotland's bleak mists. Chief Stoker Rump had been in the *Castile* during the Invergordon mutiny in the early thirties, when the ship's companies had refused orders to sail for the southern ports until a pay dispute had been settled. A right rumpus that had been, he said, but it had all come to little enough in the end, though the ringleaders had suffered the consequences of folly. Chief Petty Officer Froggett had been in the ship with a light cruiser squadron of the Mediterranean Fleet in Malta the time when the *Royal Oak* court martials had taken place, the rear-admiral commanding a battle squadron having called the Royal Marine bandmaster a bastard, though there was some doubt about the exact nomenclature since the bandmaster's name happened to be Percy Barnacle. The rear-admiral's name had been Collard, the same officer who, as a lieutenant, had been said to have caused a semi-mutiny in Pompey barracks by giving the order to the stoker division, on the parade ground: 'On your knees, you dogs,' an order and a rumpus that had led to the parade ground being publicly disgraced by the erection of a high fence to screen further outrages from the civvies . . . .

It was all naval talk, naturally enough; had the drinkers been younger men, it would have ended in naval songs as well, but they all held responsible jobs aboard and didn't wish to chance their arms if things got riotous and attracted the attention of the naval patrols pacing up and down Queen Street and Edinburgh Road and Commercial Road, the closer purlieus of the barracks and dockyard. The patrols were always on the watch for trouble, they were a darn sight worse than the civvy police, and it was the custom for the officer of the patrol to walk ahead of his men so that any rating who failed to salute him could be nabbed by the patrol behind, reported to his ship or establishment, and shoved in the rattle – Commander's Report – for failing to salute an officer.

Chief Petty Officer Shine left the party early but not early enough to catch the last bus out to Rowlands Castle. Never mind: there was the train. He walked through to the Town Station by the Guildhall, passing one of the patrols. As he went for the low-level platforms and the stopping train to Waterloo there was something of a fracas involving the station patrol and the naval Railway Transport Officer: a rating from the *Castile* seemed to be the cause of it, a man Shine recognized. Ordinary Seaman MacTavish, known to his mates as Haggis, one of the six-inch-gun's crews and cack-handed as a sack, which was why he was immediately recognizable to the chief gunner's mate, who halted in his stride for a look-see. MacTavish was very drunk, weaving around on his feet and shouting in his Scottish accent, something about effing Sassenachs. Drunk and cack-handed he might be, but he wasn't a bad lad for a Hostilities-Only rating, and he was a *Castile*, which meant a lot to Bullshit Shine.

He went forward.

'Just a minute,' he said to the leading seaman of the patrol. 'What's the trouble?'

'Drunk and being a nuisance, Chief.'

'And a disgrace to the ship and all,' Shine said to Ordinary Seaman MacTavish, who belched but offered no other comment. Shine was about to speak again when the RTO's duty officer emerged from his office with the officer of the station patrol, both of them middle-aged lieutenants RN which pre-supposed they were ex lower deck. One of them said briskly, 'What's all this about, then?'

Shine stepped forward and saluted. 'One o' mine, sir.'

'Not your business, though, Chief.'

Shine said stubbornly, 'I'd like to make it so, sir.'

The lieutenant looked at Shine's lapel badges, crossed guns with a crown above and a star below, all in gold lace. 'Chief gunner's mate . . . one of your gun's-crews, is he?'

'Yes, sir.'

'So what are you suggesting, Chief?'

'Leave 'im to me, sir.'

'Protecting your ship's name.'

'You might may so, sir, yes.'

'What'd you do with him?'

'Take 'im to Aggie Weston's, sir.' Shine's reference was to the Royal Sailors' Rest just up Commercial Road, opposite the end of Edinburgh Road, handy for the barracks and the dockyard – one of three such hostels in the home ports, Chatham, Devonport and Portsmouth, established by a certain Miss Agnes Weston about the turn of the century. Aggie Weston's was teetotal within its portals but was broadminded as to what its overnight residents had consumed prior to admission: Miss Weston's objective had been to help sailors rather than to moralize. 'They'll cope, sir.'

The lieutenant rubbed a fleshy jaw then said, 'All right. I don't want to run matlows in if there's an alternative. It's up to you, Chief.'

'Thank you, sir.' Shine saluted again, then took MacTavish by the collar. 'You – march,' he said. 'Don't give any bloody trouble, or else.' He propelled the Scot out of the station and turned to the right through the blackout and the crowds of libertymen. MacTavish lurched but gave no bother and no lip: the chief gunner's mate was a VIP aboard any ship and Shine could be a bastard when he wanted to be. Now, he was having a sobering effect. By the time Shine had handed over his burden to the night porter at Aggie Weston's, he'd missed the last train as well as the last bus. He wouldn't get home that night. Walk it? Not likely, take all night. Rosie his wife wasn't on the phone; the local village bobby was, of course, and Shine fished in his pocket for some coppers and rang from a telephone kiosk. Pc Bottram would get on his bike and pedal up Redhill Road from the Green. In this war, men in uniform stood together and helped out.

Shine cursed to himself: sentimental, that was his trouble. What he wouldn't do for the old *Castile*! But Rosie would understand because like him she was married to the navy. And come tomorrow, Ordinary Seaman MacTavish would be feeling the rough edge of his tongue.

iv

A number of the other senior ratings from those earlier commissions had lived in Pompey, naturally for men of the Portsmouth Port Division, and most of them had remained in the town after going out on pension because that was where their mates were and because in a naval port ex-naval men tended to get priority when looking for jobs. They were known to be trustworthy and the Post Office wasn't the only employer who recognized their value. Some got work in the dockyard, others found jobs as bank guards

23

or messengers. Unlike Chief PO Shine, not all of them had moved out of Pompey on the outbreak of war. There were various reasons for this. In the case of Yeoman of Signals Robbins it was because his wife had died and he had no home of his own to worry about. Dorothy had been run down by a Corporation bus aboard which he had been the conductor, a trolley bus going round the corner by the Royal Pier Hotel opposite Victoria Barracks. There had been a scream and a lurch and Robbins had got down in a panic and found it was Dorothy. The scene was etched on his mind, ineradicably, all of it: the inert body, his driver with his head in his hands, the shocked faces of the people who had stopped to watch, ghoul-like, even the minor details, the blue sky with streaks of white cloud, cars stopped on the other side of the road, a policeman materializing from nowhere, the horror on the face of the sentry at the barrack gate, a private of the King's Own Scottish Borderers with trews, pipe-clayed belt, and rifle, who for no useful reason had called out the quarter-guard. Then the ambulance, and temporary oblivion for Robbins, who had fainted.

After the funeral he had cleared up the little house in a road off Arundel Street and moved in with Dorothy's married sister in Cosham at the northern end of the city. She'd married well, a solicitor's clerk, and had enough room, but of course it wasn't really home although he'd been made very welcome. He had left the buses and got a job with the Southern Railway at Fratton goods yards, hoping that with his naval experience he might get a transfer to signalman. But he hadn't been really interested: Dorothy's death had left him with one wish: to get back to the *Andrew* and forget in the wastes of the sea. He had taken steps to be accepted by the Royal Fleet Auxiliaries as a signalman in a fleet oiler when Hitler had marched into Poland and he got his recall to the navy and obeyed the summons with alacrity.

Tonight, he left the public house in Queen Street and

caught a bus out to Cosham. Dorothy's sister, Maggie, wasn't in: her two boys were. 'Dad's been taken ill,' the elder one said. 'Mum's gone to the hospital.'

'I'm sorry, lad,' Robbins said. 'What's up with your dad, then?'

'I – I don't know.' The boy's lips were trembling. 'He had a bad pain in his stomach . . . .'

'Appendix, maybe. Nothing to get worried about. Which hospital, Royal or St. Mary's?'

'Royal.'

'I'll get round there,' Robbins said. 'Your mum'll want someone with her, I reckon. You two'll be all right, eh?'

The boy nodded. 'Yes, Uncle Jack.'

Robbins left the house. No more buses, and a long walk back through North End almost to the Edinburgh Road turning off Commercial Road, right through the blackout. A sorry ending to a happy night with his mates. Maggie in trouble and the *Castile* likely to be under sailing orders any time now. Robbins didn't really believe that Fred Purkiss had appendicitis. According to Maggie, he'd had a lot of trouble with his stomach recently and his face had gone a nasty shade of yellow and he'd lost a good deal of weight, so that his clothes hung from him like a scarecrow.

As Yeoman of Signals Robbins turned in at the entrance to the Royal Portsmouth Hospital Chief Stoker Rump, one of those who didn't live in Pompey any more but had moved to Newcastle where his wife came from, was engaged in barter a little way down Queen Street from the public house. Drink, he had found, always had a certain effect on his desires, and a young woman had accosted him.

'Jiggy-jig?'

Rump halted. 'How much?'

'Short time five bob.'

Chief Stoker Rump didn't want to go back aboard, nor did he want to go to Aggie Weston's. 'All night?'

'Ten bob.'

Rump felt in his pocket. 'Seven-and-a tanner do?'

'Mean bugger, aren't you?' The voice was shrill.

'All I got. An' that's the best part of a day's pay. Take it or leave it, girl.'

'Sod off.' She turned her shoulder. Rump was about to settle for five bob's worth when she moved away and came beneath the unkind light of a moon that had emerged suddenly from behind cloud. Talk about haggard . . . lined face and dank, greasy hair. Rump let his fistful of coins drop back into his pocket, feeling salvation and the timely hand of God as he continued on towards the main gate of the dockyard and his virginal hammock aboard the *Castile*. In this war and its blackout, many a matlow had struck a bum bargain, paid in advance as they mostly demanded, and then seen the truth too late in the harsh electric light of a sleazy room.

When Chief Stoker Rump put a leg out of his hammock next morning, the buzz was already strong: *Castile* was leaving port in the forenoon of the following day and all night leave was cancelled.

v

The rain that had come as the ship was unberthing stayed with them, a very dirty day with a wind now blowing up from the south-west. The men on watch on the bridge and at the guns, half the armament manned in cruising stations, huddled in oilskins and duffel coats, the hoods of the latter pulled over their heads, their minds filled with thoughts of past, present and future. The homes they had left, their families, and what was in store for them as the ship moved west, passing Cowes and then the great rocky jags of the Needles, leaving Southampton Water away on the starboard quarter, a Southampton now mostly empty of the great passenger liners under requisition as troop transports and based on northern waters – the Clyde, close to Ordinary Seaman MacTavish's home in Glasgow. MacTavish came from the Gorbals, toughest of tough

26

areas, where the police patrolled in pairs and were all big men, very different from the police in the soft south, and with bull's faces to match. The Gorbals was the home of the knife, the sandbag, the knuckleduster and the sharp-filed bicycle chain, plus other nasties. In peacetime MacTavish, especially when drunk, would have made short work of Chief Petty Officer Shine, but by now he had hoisted in the power of naval discipline and the inadvisability of bucking it, the more so when it came in the shape of Bullshit Shine, who though small was a terror and epitomized the Naval Discipline Act and the Articles of War, the latter being in part a catalogue of the navy's crimes and their punishments. When these had first been routinely read over to Ordinary Seaman MacTavish, he had gathered that each and every crime gave a Commanding Officer the option to order that the miscreant should suffer death. The fact that the word death was followed by the more comforting option 'or such other punishment as is hereinafter mentioned' didn't entirely obliterate death in MacTavish's Gorbals-oriented mind and he was fairly certain that to thrust his seaman's knife into Bullshit Shine would be regarded as extreme. So, the morning after, when he shambled out of Aggie Weston's and reported back aboard, and had been button-holed by the chief gunners mate, he had minded his Ps and Qs.

'Ordinary Seaman MacTavish.'

'Aye . . . .'

'Aye, *Chief.*'

'Aye, Chief.'

'Lousy little sod.' Shine's direct stare bored into him like a drill. 'Bringing the ship into disrepute. Getting drunk's one thing and there's plenty of us as has done that in the past, stand fast the God botherers. Fighting drunk and shouting the odds, that's different. I won't have the *Castile* let down – got it ?' Shine was like a terrier with its hackles up. MacTavish loomed over him, some five inches taller but totally subdued by the sheer energy and personality of the

27

chief gunner's mate. 'Next time it happens, if I see you, Ordinary Seaman MacTavish, I'll run you in myself the moment you get back aboard. That's if I haven't bloody *killed* you first, which I'd have a good mind to. Right?'

'Aye, Chief.'

'So watch it.' Shine shifted tack. 'What's that round your neck?'

'Scarf.'

'I know it's a bloody scarf, I got eyes. Scarfs is all right as rig o' the day at sea in wartime but they have to be *blue*.' MacTavish's was red. 'Take it off, pronto.'

'But I – '

'Pronto I said.'

MacTavish removed the offending article, muttering to himself as the chief gunner's mate turned about and marched away. A popsie had given MacTavish that bright red scarf last time he was on leave in Glasgow and he treasured it. Besides, it was warm and he'd lost his blue one . . . he moved on aft towards the quarter-deck, glowering. Roll on the end of the war, he thought.

He wasn't the only one thinking that as the *Castile* headed westerly, destination unknown to everyone aboard apart from the Captain, the navigator and the First Lieutenant, John Brown. Most of the Hostilities-Only ratings couldn't wait to get back to their normal lives, to pick up the threads that had been broken back in September 1939. They were of all backgrounds – clerks and salesmen, teachers, bricklayers and painters, shop assistants, actors, writers, solicitors, all thrown together to live the hard life of the lower deck, living in broadside messes that in the smaller ships were mostly awash in anything of a sea as the little escorts shepherded the big ships of the vital convoys across the North Atlantic, past the North Cape to Russian ports, or through the Mediterranean to Malta during the long months of the siege when the garrison and the people were largely down to eating rats until the relieving convoys came in to lift their spirits for a while. Some of the HO ratings were what were known as CW candidates, those with recommends for a commission and now doing their qualifying sea time before going to HMS *King Alfred* for officer training, partly in Lancing College in Sussex and partly in what was to have been the new swimming bath complex in Hove. One of these was Ordinary Seaman Quentin, only recently called up on reaching the age of twenty. In civilian life he had been an undergraduate at King's College, Cambridge, reading law. His mates thought him stuck-up, toffee-nosed, but he couldn't help it. You couldn't shift mentally from a Cambridge college to the lower deck of a warship as fast as all that. He did try, however, though it was almost worse when he did, since they thought him condescending. They called him Fatarse, in clear reference to a quirk of his anatomy, and he just had to put up with it.

'You, Fatarse.' This was Leading Seaman Pafford, keen, efficient and young, not one of the Fleet Reserve dugouts.

'Yes, killick?'

'Move yourself ! Ship's at sea in case you didn't know. Get up off your bum, report to the forebridge. One of the lookouts took sick, which 'as fucked the Watch and Quarter Bill. Sooner you get there the better so 'e can go down to the quack.'

The *Castile* was rolling badly now as she came past the Needles, and Quentin was unhandy in a seaway. He went up the bridge ladder like a crab, holding on with all claws. He heard the laughter drifting up from below: Fatarse was a sight for sore eyes, all right.

The First Lieutenant turned away from a conversation with the Captain as Quentin reached the bridge and saluted.

'Name?' the First Lieutenant asked briskly.

'Quentin, sir.' They hadn't all learned names yet: the new commission was only a couple of weeks old, and ordinary seamen were small enough fry.

'Right, Quentin. Take over starboard lookout, sweep from dead ahead to 090 degrees.'

'Yes, sir.'

'Repeat the order, Quentin.'

'Yes, sir. Starboard lookout, sir, sweep from dead ahead to the beam.' He felt proud of that.

'Very clever, Quentin but not what I said. I said to 090 degrees. Keep your eyes skinned, report anything you see. And I mean anything.'

The ship moved on, passing along England's south coast. There was no more conversation between Captain and First Lieutenant. John Brown was edgy: first time under RNVR command, and the implications of the knowledge, so far little enough certainly, that he had been given of the *Castile*'s orders didn't bring any uplift to the spirit. Far from it.

3

JOHN BROWN, lieutenant RN ex lower deck, was now aboard a *Castile* that was the same but different. Physically the light cruiser was much as she had been on the China station in 1937, the only obtrusive differences being the removal of the torpedo tubes and the addition of radar aerials and more up-to-date WT equipment and the change in the main armament. But in other respects the change had been great. In the 1930s the gulf between lower deck and wardroom was enormous, much greater than now with the wartime relaxation of the former bullshit, a relaxation inevitably brought about by the influx of RNR and RNVR officers, to say nothing of the Hostilities-Only ratings who were a different breed from the pre-war pusser RN ratings.

John Brown had joined the service as a seaman boy second class and trained at HMS *Ganges*, the shore establishment at Shotley in Suffolk. At *Ganges* everything was done at the double, and the chief gunner's mate of the parade was a martinet, a sort of non-commissioned God, actual God being the Captain, a remote figure who inspected the divisions on Sundays before church, resplendent in frock coat with four gold stripes on either cuff. At the boats the chief seamanship instructor was rather less of a martinet but yet saw that every last bit of slackness was pounced upon with a degree of apparent ferocity largely engendered just to impress green youth with

31

the necessity of getting things right since men's lives were interdependent at sea.

Then there had been the mast.

The great mast that reared heavenwards from the edge of the parade ground, its yards draped with the foot-ropes, its tops rearing above the futtock shrouds and the lubber's hole through which it was reckoned cowardly to pass. You had, if you were any good, to climb those outward-leaning futtock shrouds, your body bent backwards as your feet felt for the rope rungs, high above the tarmac. Seaman Boy Second Class John Brown had been the youngest ever to climb to the truck, and stand there with arms folded, looking down an immense distance to the ground. He seemed to have nerves of steel.

Passing out as an ordinary seaman, John Brown was rated AB in quick time, and in quick time made leading seaman. As such he had joined the old *Castile* in Pompey dockyard and had sailed away to join the China Squadron in Hong Kong. His memories of the commission were vivid and abiding: a happy ship as she had always been. Cruises up the China coast, to Shanghai and Wei-hai-Wei; exercises off Hong Kong, shoots and dummy torpedo runs, plenty of sport ashore. The occasional trauma of a typhoon when boats had been stove in by the force of wind and water, funnels carried away, gun-mountings twisted and so on. Ashore, as well as sport there had been women and John Brown was a vigorous man who took his opportunities gladly. Before leaving Pompey he'd heard stories from old China hands: Chinese women were different between the legs. Instead of fore-and-aft it went athwartships. John Brown had disproved that quickly enough, but had fallen like his mentors under the spell of young, very young, Chinese womanhood. They knew what it was there for and they knew how to please a man. There had been many times when after night leave John Brown had returned shagged out but never had he allowed his weariness to show or to affect his duty as a leading hand. He was hard-working, efficient, fair but firm.

32

His divisional officer in those days had been quick to spot the potential and sent for him during an afternoon siesta when the ship was alongside in Victoria Harbour, Hong Kong.

'I've had my eye on you, Brown.'

'Sir!' Leading Seaman Brown, rigid at attention with his cap held against his left thigh, had had a bad moment, though he could think of nothing left undone.

'You come of a naval family. Your father.'

'Yessir. Both grand-dads too, sir.'

'Really? Something to be proud of, Brown. I've no doubt you are.'

'Yessir.'

'I see from your parchment that your father was a chief PO. Your grandfathers?'

'One o' them was PO First Class, sir. Seaman branch, of course, like my dad.' The officer had hidden a smile at the clear reference to the superiority of the seaman branch above all others. 'And my mum's father, he was a leading seaman. Served in the old Sail Training Squadron, sir.'

'Quite a tradition. Well, you'll be wondering what all this is about, Brown.'

'Yessir.' Don't look at an officer, look away above his head: to stare direct was insubordination. Brown's gaze travelled through the port towards the shore where the Chinese girls lurked and soon he would be watch ashore again.

'You've impressed me, Brown. The Captain and Commander as well. Ever thought of applying for Upper Yardman?'

Brown was shaken rigid for a moment. 'Me, sir?'

'I'm not addressing anyone else, Brown.'

'Nossir. Sorry, sir. Well, sir.'

'Well what?'

'Lower deck, sir. My family, like. Wardrooms, they....'

'Nonsense. This is the nineteen-thirties, not the eighteen-nineties. You know the routine for Upper Yardmen.'

Leading Seaman Brown did, by hearsay anyway. A draft back to the depot in his present rate, a lot of parade-ground stuff to develop power of command plus a lot of grooming to instil social tittery into a common seaman. Under eagle eyes the whole time, any slips and you were out, back to the fleet and the messdecks. If you made the grade then they commissioned you as mate with one gold stripe like a sub-lieutenant but not yet fully promoted to that rank while you were watched and assessed again. When you passed that hurdle, then you were a proper sub-lieutenant with your officer career before you. A little old for the further promotion stakes but you could get places right enough. At least one ex lower deck man had made Commander just recently to John Brown's knowledge.

He felt much flattered and accepted the offer of a recommend and hoped for the best. The Captain had forwarded an application and in the end he'd made it, though at thirty-one now he was old for a two-striper and still had four years to go for his half stripe as lieutenant-commander. He was envious of the RNVR such as Cameron, who could get acting rank and by-pass the strict RN time schedule for promotion. But Lieutenant Brown had never ceased being grateful to the old *Castile* for having given him his big chance. He had thrown himself into the war effort with dedication. He had seen action of a sort early on, being a survivor of the sinking of the *Royal Oak*, torpedoed by a U-boat that had crept through the boom at Scapa in the old battleship's wake. This and a few early sinkings apart – the liner *Athenia* with women and children aboard, and the aircraft carrier *Courageous* among others – little had seemed to be happening during the 'phoney war' period that had lasted from September 1939 until the German attack on Holland and Belgium in the May of 1940; and Brown's relative inaction had ended at Dunkirk, when he'd been a sub-lieutenant in one of the relieving destroyers.

Now, aboard the *Castile* once again, he was bound for

Scapa and memories of a dreadful Saturday night and the screams of trapped and wounded men aboard the *Royal Oak*.

Scapa: a naval canteen where you could get a limit of two pints of Brickwood's beer brought up from Pompey, sheep, snow and ice and biting winds, wartime home as it seemed for half the navy. You could keep it. But they were not going to be there long.

ii

'It's a red herring,' Cameron had said in the privacy of his cabin the night before the *Castile* sailed from Portsmouth. 'Just to fool the German naval command. Our objective's a long way from Scapa. There's a strong need to lull suspicions. While we're in Scapa certain work will be carried out aboard, structural work – dockyard mateys have been sent up from Portsmouth for the purpose. Too many potential prying eyes down south or it would have been done here in the dockyard, of course.'

It had been John Brown who had asked what the final objective was.

'I'm not at liberty to say yet, Number One. You'll know just as soon as I can tell you. Meanwhile, what I've already said is to go no further – that's understood?'

There were three assents: Hugh Batten the navigator, an RNR lieutenant, peacetime second officer in the Canadian Pacific liners; the First Lieutenant, and the engineer officer.

'Gin?' Cameron suggested. There was unanimous agreement. The Captain's steward, summoned by the press of a button, poured the gin, taken with plain water as was the naval custom, and returned to his pantry with his glass-cloth over his arm, somewhat chokker because he hadn't managed to overhear anything and it was expected of any captain's steward that he kept his ears well a-flap for the edification of the ship's company, just so that they had some idea of what lay in store. Buzzes were the lifeblood in

35

wartime and you always, naturally, hoped to hear something nice though you seldom did.

The gin drunk and no refills offered, the officers dispersed. Lieutenant(E) Rogers went below to make some pre-sailing checks with his chief engine-room artificer, Chief PO Hollyman, like himself an old *Castile* hand. Rogers' memories were of the Med Fleet in peacetime, under the overall command of Admiral Sir William Fisher, a man of sidewhiskers and an unorthodox, relaxed approach, an admiral much liked in the Mediterranean who had died subsequently when Commander-in-Chief Portsmouth, catching a cold while taking the salute at a gale-swept King's birthday parade on Southsea Common when in his early sixties. Malta in peacetime, Gibraltar in peacetime, had been superb : days of sunshine and sparkling sea mostly though the weather could on occasions be as bad as anywhere else . . . dances in the evenings beneath the spread awnings with a marine or bluejacket's band playing, and women in plenty, both married and single, and the married ones often enough with husbands at sea and themselves very available for the assuagement of their desires – more so than the single girls who wouldn't take risks and who in any case were heavily chaperoned by forbidding mothers or aunts or old family friends . . . .

'A penny for 'em, sir,' CERA Hollyman said with a grin. He knew Rogers and the way his mind drifted towards the fleshpots : he had happened to be Chief ERA with him in another ship in Malta, when Rogers had been a sub-lieutenant.

Rogers returned the grin. 'You're too young, Chief.' They had made their tour of inspection and were yarning up top, outside the air-lock that led down to the engine spaces. Hollyman scratched at his grey hairs and said he wished he was.

'You're never too old, Chief.'

'Doesn't come any easier, sir, put it that way. The popsies, they just think you're a sort of sea-daddy.' Rogers, he thought, might as well make the most of his youth: he was a well-set-up young officer, handsome and outgoing with an engaging grin and Hollyman wished him luck. He went on to say, after a pause, that there had been something on his mind: the ship was full of old *Castiles*.

'Funny, don't you think, sir?'

'Oh, I don't know, Chief. Coincidence.'

'Not much coincidence in the Drafting Office, sir. Them Drafting Jaunties, they know what they're doing and its mostly bloody evil. Like drafting a bloke to Hong Kong when his old mum's at death's door.'

'That sounded heartfelt, Chief. You didn't – '

'Heartfelt it was, sir. Happened to me. My old mum, she was in 'ospital with an ulcer, but the sods packed me off China-side. Not this ship, the old *Kent*. Never got over that, I didn't.'

'I'm not surprised. But I doubt if there's anything evil this time, Chief.'

'I don't know so much,' Hollyman said darkly. He semi-echoed the earlier thoughts of Mr Marty: 'It's like a wake, sir. All the family gathered in.'

Rogers looked at him, frowning. 'I see your point. But I wouldn't express the thought too much. You know what sailors are, Chief.'

'Yes, sir. Superstitious buggers, sir.' He excused himself and turned away. He still had jobs to see to.

iii

Castile had turned up around Land's End, between the Wolf Rock and the Scillies, thereafter standing clear of the Cornish coast to leave the Bristol Channel to starboard as she headed for the Small Rocks light off St Bride's Bay and Milford Haven, thence to enter St George's Channel for the Irish Sea. As they made their northing Cameron swept the seas through his binoculars, adding his eyes to those of the bridge lookouts. They were in enclosed waters sure enough, but the ubiquitous U-boats had strong penetrative qualities and there was always the possibility of a feather of spray from a periscope. The wind and rain had gone now, and the sea was flat, and it should not be hard to spot the first indication of attack.

Cameron brought his glasses down. 'Peaceful enough, Pilot,' he remarked.

'Yes, sir. Nothing on the Asdic, anyway.'

Cameron listed to the pinging sound coming from the Asdic cabinet, a monotonous sound but one that tended after so many years of war to fade into the background of consciousness, at any rate until the note changed on picking up an echo. As Cameron turned to watch the coast of South Wales slide past there was a report from one of the lookouts.

'Vessel, sir, fine on the port bow.'

'Thank you, Norton.' Glasses up to the eyes again: a smudge of smoke that became an armed trawler. Within the next minute she was signalling the day's identification letters. 'Coastal convoy out of Belfast for Milford Haven I expect,' Cameron said. 'Yeoman, make the reply.'

'Aye, aye, sir.' Leading Signalman Wallace, yeoman of the watch, aimed his Aldis lamp and flashed the response. A moment later the trawler made its signal letters and Wallace reported, '*Foxtrot*, sir.' Behind the little trawler the ships of the convoy could be seen, around thirty or forty of them, with more armed trawlers out on the beams to port and starboard. A lot of smoke was being made and to Cameron's eye the ships looked all over the place, the columns mixed up in a way that the ocean convoys seldom were. It was natural enough, with ships of so many different types and tonnages. Messages were exchanged with the trawler escort leader, and the *Castile* moved on towards the Skerries outside Liverpool Bay and the Mersey. As later they came past the Skerries light Cameron and the navigator were still on the bridge. Hugh Batten looked with nostalgia towards the distant entry to the port of Liverpool

38

astride the Mersey. That was where he had sailed from in the Canadian Pacific liners, and his home was on the outskirts of Liverpool. Had been, that was: Goering's *Luftwaffe* had taken it out along with a number of other houses, just as though it had never been there at all, and Batten's wife and two small children had simply ceased to be, along with his home. Valerie had intended taking the children to Batten's parents in Bolton-by-Bowland up in Lancashire, shutting up the home for the duration, but she'd left it too late. Batten's feelings in regard to the Nazis could scarcely be expressed; but now he prayed that whatever the *Castile*'s mission was to be, it would involve something that would ease his anger a little in terms of the sheer satisfaction of revenge.

Below on the fo'c'sle Chief PO Froggett, chief bosun's mate, otherwise known as the buffer, glanced up at the forebridge and saw Batten behind the glass screen. Looking across at Liverpool, he was, and Froggett knew why. Froggett's home also was near Liverpool, and it was so far intact – far enough out, he believed, to be safe. The two men, coming from the Pool as had soon emerged, had talked as townies a few days earlier and the facts had come out.

'Poor bloke,' Froggett said to Leading Seaman Pafford.

'Who, buff?'

'Navvy. Mr Batten.'

'Why?'

Froggett told him. Pafford shrugged and said, 'Not the only one, is he?'

'Not saying he is. Doesn't make it any less, does it?'

'S'pose not. Daft place to live, though – Liverpool.'

'His home port in the liners. Besides, I live there too.'

Pafford grinned: Froggett thought he had an unpleasant face when he grinned. So many of the up-and-coming young leading hands and petty officers were the same – kind of ruthless, too pusser, too anxious to impress by a show of hardness. His own generation had been at the same time tougher and more human, kinder and more tolerant of, say, green young ordinary seamen. Pafford said, 'Sorry I spoke, buff.'

'Forget it,' Froggett said, and moved aft. It was getting on time for the pipe Up Spirits, when the rum issue would be broken out and measured off for the messes in the presence of a regulating PO, the PO of the Day which was Froggett, and an officer. Today the officer was Sub-Lieutenant Calcott, an RNVR and still wet behind the ears like an OD. He needed nursing along, and Froggett was a good nurse, a regular sea daddy in spite of a craggy face and a jaw like the Bass Rock in the Firth of Forth.

Froggett, as the pipe came over the Tannoy, made for the spirit room. Mr Calcott was there already, scared of being late, and looking a little green in the face – there was a swell coming out from Liverpool Bay and Calcott hadn't quite got his sea legs, and the smell of rum, once the barricoes were broken out, would be very strong.

'Best not breathe in, sir,' Froggett said. 'Many a matlow's got drunk on the aroma alone.'

'Has he really, Chief?'

Froggett looked at him. Subby would believe anything of the sea. 'Well, sir, no, not really. Not that I knows of anyway.' He hoped Calcott wouldn't puke his guts up over the rum issue; that would go down badly with the ship's company and subby would never be allowed to forget. When the RPO broke out the spirit and drew it from the barricoe with the copper pump, saw it watered and measured out for each mess from his list of those who drew it rather than take the threepence a day in lieu – paid to the men shown on the ship's books as T for Temperance instead of G for Grog, or UA for Under Age – the smell was like a knife. A kindly knife in Froggett's view . . . but Calcott's face grew greener and he began to sweat and swallow. But he held onto his stomach by some miracle and when the measuring was complete he managed to give the customary order in regard to the inevitable leavings.

40

'Throw it in the scuppers, PO.'

The RPO said automatically, 'Aye, aye, sir.' The order was a yardarm-clearer: once given, the responsibility was no longer the officer's. The RPO left the spirit room with the jug of leavings, which would go down his own throat in due course. Or so he thought. But subby called him back.

'I – I'm supposed to see it thrown away, PO,' he said.

A look of studied amazement came to the RPO's features. 'Is that so, sir?'

'It's laid down . . . in King's Regulations and Admiralty – '

Well, sir, it's as you say, o' course, sir,' the RPO said frigidly. Watched by Calcott, the precious fluid was carried away and poured into the scuppers to flow down into the hogwash. Afterwards, the RPO had much to say to Froggett. 'Never heard the like in all my life I haven't . . . I only wish Mr Marty could be permanent Up Spirits duty, 'e knows what's what! Young bleeder . . . Up Spirits, eh – talk about Stand Fast the 'Oly Ghost!'

'Only doing his duty,' Froggett said. 'He'll learn.'

'Fucking RNVR.'

iv

Sub-Lieutenant Calcott knew he'd pulled a bit of a boner by being over-pusser: the RPO had made that plain enough in his manner. But he *had* done his duty and he meant to be a conscientious officer now that His Majesty the King had seen fit to give him a commission, which he didn't give to everybody. Before joining the navy as an ordinary seaman, Calcott had worked in a bank, a very junior clerk in great awe of his manager, who had also had an expressive face though with a pernickety manner. He had been an indefatigable fault-finder. Rumour had it that he was hen-pecked by a massive wife at home and thus took it out on his subordinates at the bank. His constant theme had been duty: duty to the customer, duty to the bank. Leave not a jot undone. Learn all the customers' signatures and never err. Attend the counter the moment a customer entered – no-one must be kept waiting. Add and subtract correctly and bring all overdrafts to the immediate attention of the chief cashier. Be ready to provide a statement the second it was asked for. Never, never attempt to cover up an error. Tell the truth, confess misdemeanours. Do your duty to the full at all times.

Excellent strictures, of course. But the manager had left nothing to Calcott's own initative to sort out the sheep from the goats. So he had learned above all to stick rigidly to the rules come what may. Which was what he had just done in the spirit room.

From the scupper episode he went along to the wardroom, ready for an early lunch before reporting to the bridge to take over the afternoon watch at 1200 hours, relieving the gunnery officer, Peter Blake, another RNVR. Whilst in coastal waters the Officer of the Watch was in fact something of a spare number, a dogsbody, since both the Captain and the navigator were usually present, or anyway one of them was, relieving each other for meals and so on. The First Lieutenant came into the wardroom as Calcott sat in a big leather armchair near the high fender that surrounded the wardroom fireplace. Calcott got to his feet.

Brown waved a hand. 'Sit down, sub. We don't stand on ceremony.' He sat himself on the fender's wide leather top and looked hard at Calcott. 'Anything up, is there?'

'No . . . no, sir. Not really.'

'That means there is. Out with it, lad.'

'Yes, sir.' Tell the truth, the manager's words coming back from the past. Calcott said what he had done and that the RPO hadn't seemed pleased.

Brown concealed a smile. 'You were quite right, of course. Never let it be said to the contrary! The RPO will be a shade wary of you in future, and that's no bad thing. On the other hand . . . .'

'Yes, sir?'

'The blind eye can be useful in small matters. There are such things in the Andrew as perks attaching to certain ranks and ratings, and those concerned don't like them interfered with. If the RPO got blotto on his perks, that'd be a different matter. But he won't ever do that. Get the point, sub?'

Calcott nodded. There was more to being a fully fledged naval officer than he had been taught at *King Alfred*. However, he was here to learn, and learn he would, as Chief PO Froggett, out of his hearing, had said. But – and this also Calcott didn't know – there was going to be scant time left for learning as HMS *Castile* steamed towards Armageddon.

4

Passing through the North Channel between the Firth of Clyde and the Northern Irish coast, coming between the Mull of Kintyre and Rathlin Island in the afternoon watch of a deteriorating day, the *Castile* headed up towards Islay, and Skerryvore, and in due course the Minches for Cape Wrath. Thence she would make the passage north about for the Pentland Firth between Duncansby Head on the Scottish mainland and the Old Man of Hoy to enter Switha Sound and anchor in the destroyer anchorage off the naval base on Hoy opposite Long Hope. On entry around noon next day she passed by the old battleship *Iron Duke,* formerly Admiral Jellicoe's flagship in the Grand Fleet of the previous war, now cemented to the sea bottom after attack by German aircraft early in the current war and used as an accommodation ship for officers and men in transit, waiting to join ships as they came in from sea.

'Thank God for that,' Chief Stoker Rump said as the judder throughout the ship indicated the letting go of an anchor. The latter part of the run north had been a filthy one, and there was a lot of water along the messdecks, some of it having seeped into the sanctity of the petty officers' mess. 'Next thing's a pint of Brickwood's in the canteen, I reckon. That's if leave's piped.' No-one answered him: Chief Stoker Rump was known to natter

44

away to himself and didn't always expect interruption: mostly you just saw his lips move, since the racket in the engine spaces and the roar of the furnaces in the boiler-rooms deadened all other sound. It was a curious sensation when the skipper rang down Finished With Engines and the noise stopped, like another world, a sane one where a man could think straight.

Soon after anchoring, the First Lieutenant approached Cameron. 'D'you intend to pipe shore liberty, sir?'

'If anyone wants to go ashore in this.' Rainwater streamed from Cameron's oilskin and there was a blow, quite a strong one, but the weather reports had indicated that it would moderate by nightfall, which was around 2100 hours in the north latitudes at this time of year.

'You know matlows, sir. Anything for the shore.'

'Yes. All right, Number One. You can pipe leave from 1600 to 2200 for the non-duty watch. You can use both motor-cutters to land libertymen at 1600 and 1700, boats off shore to leave the pier at 2100 and 2200.'

'Aye, aye, sir.' Brown hesitated. 'You going ashore yourself?'

'Not bloody likely! I'll catch up on some sleep.'

'Right, sir. Permission to stretch my legs?'

Cameron grinned. 'By all means – sooner you than me!' Then he added, 'I want enough executive officers aboard to maintain an anchor watch, Number One, at least until the wind moderates. See to that, will you? And steam at immediate notice.'

'Yes, sir.' Brown turned away and went down the ladder to the upper deck. Wind meant a ship could drag its anchor and find herself ashore with the libertymen, or bashing around the anchorage as a menace to all other ships. Thus you kept a full bridge watch and had your engines ready either to steam up to the anchor to keep the weight of cable on the bottom or to up anchor and away out to sea where there was room to manoeuvre. When that happened, libertymen could get left ashore until the ship came back in,

45

and Scapa wasn't the most hospitable place in the world. Brown went ashore in the first libertyboat, taking his walking stick with him, still wearing oilskin and seaboots. He could stride out and commune with the sheep that would be skulking behind the low stone walls and windbreaks, seeking shelter in advance of the fresh snow that Brown believed was coming and never mind the weather reports. The sky, which was low, had a heavy grey look tinged with red.

As he walked, he wondered what the final orders would be. All Cameron had said so far was that they were to shift tomorrow at first light into the floating dock that was anchored in the comparative shelter of two headlands forming an enclosed bay. There, they would receive the attentions of the dockyard mateys, currently accommodated aboard the *Iron Duke*, for what purpose would be revealed shortly. Once they started work, so would the galley wireless, busy with buzzes.

Brown was thinking of his wife at home in Fareham near Portsmouth. Never mind his dedication to the service, he'd hated leaving her. He'd been married only a little more than a year; the advancement of his career had left him little time for thoughts of matrimony and he would need the marriage allowance which was not payable before the age of thirty; but when he'd met Evelyn he had fallen deeply in love – somewhat hopelessly at first, he'd thought, since her old man was a captain RN and way beyond his social class or aspirations: he still found it hard to cast off the lower deck. But all had been well, since the old man had been no snob and had seen his future son-in-law for what he was, a good officer with a future before him and much in love with his daughter.

There had been no children yet, and maybe never would be; Evelyn wasn't keen. She had her war work, for one thing: she helped to run a residential club for officers of all three services and it seemed to take up a lot of her time. Even when he was on leave, which rankled. But she was popular and said she couldn't let the job down, which he supposed was fair enough in wartime. There were officers going off to sea, there were brown jobs on leave from fighting units, there were RAF types whose lives were always on a thread. They needed their relaxation and a room for a night or so, and certainly Evelyn didn't work late when he was at home. John Brown was regretful about the lack of children: he would have liked a son. Himself, he was an only son and he would have liked to feel the Brown seafaring tradition wouldn't die with him when his time came, which in war it could at the drop of a hat. Walking through mud and slushy snow from the last fall, John Brown found some of the words of an old naval ditty running through his mind: *if it is a boy, send the bastard off to sea . . . climbing up the rigging like his daddy used to do. . . .*

That mast at the *Ganges* – so long ago now it seemed. Standing up there on the truck, looking down on the messes, or dormitories either side of the covered way, looking out across the Orwell to the port of Harwich, John Brown had felt literally on top of the world; and the years since had been good ones mostly, though he had lost a number of friends when his last ship, another light cruiser as it had happened, had gone down when escorting a convoy under heavy U-boat attack. Now he felt a dissatisfaction and was unsure whether it was to do with the uncertainty of the immediate future or with his rather neglected home in Fareham. Dust in plenty, anathema to any first lieutenant, and often dirty dishes left from one day to the next – he knew that, because he'd found them once getting week-end leave unexpectedly. But of course Evelyn couldn't be in two places at once and even though women married to serving personnel were not called up, it was expected of a lieutenant's wife who was also a captain's daughter to do war work on a voluntary basis. He couldn't really complain. . . .

Leading Seaman Slugg, acting coxwain of the 1st Motor

Cutter, had watched Brown walking away from the pier after coming alongside, watched him disappear between high banks of lying snow in the direction of Lyness.

'Pusser bugger,' he remarked to his sternsheetsman. Brown had just told Slugg off for allowing a rope's-end to be a hanging judas over the side where it could have got caught up in the Kitching steering gear : Slugg, another of the fleet reservists, didn't like being told off in front of his boat's crew who were HO to a man, except for the stoker manning the engine amidships beneath the canopy.

'Buzz says he's ex lower deck,' the sternsheetsman said.

'Yer. 'E is an' all ! They're the worst, know where to look – up to all the dodges painfully learnt from seaman boy up.' Slugg, the officer departed with the libertymen, lit a fag, a tailor-made roll-your-own from a tin of Ticklers, the navy's own cigarette tobacco, duty free like the ready-mades and preferred by Slugg because your mates didn't always like the fact you'd licked the gum on the paper so they usually refused the offer. He blew smoke that vanished fast with the wind. ''Ad a preoccupied look I thought.'

'Probably knows what we're in for.'

Slugg nodded. 'Likely, yes.'

'Any more buzzes, killick?'

'Usual tripe,' Slugg answered briefly. 'Taking the King and Queen to Canada was the last I 'eard. Little princesses an' all, safe for the duration. Or what's left of it before fuckin' 'Itler comes.'

The sternsheetsman made a jeering noise. 'They'd never cut and run, killick !'

'That's what I said. An' if they did, they'd go aboard a battle-wagon, not a titchy light cruiser that's seen the best of 'er days.'

'I thought you were soft on the *Castile* ?'

'So I am, but I'm not besotted. I see 'er limitations for a royal suite, my lad.' Leading Seaman Slugg's mind did a swift shift, back to a year or so before the war, when he'd served in the *Castile* in Pompey – on her return from foreign she'd become part of the Reserve Fleet, secured fore and aft to buoys in the upper reaches of the harbour, beyond Whale Island. It was not a distinguished period of her history and Slugg, doing his last active service job before going out on pension, had never in fact been to sea in her until now but he still had a soft spot for her. For one thing, he'd liked being shorebound for a time because he liked the Pompey scene, the Pompey bars, the Pompey women too. Slugg, who at thirty-six looked an old man and had no teeth of his own, had never married. He'd reckoned bundle men – as the old navy had known the married men on account of the bundles they carried ashore over their shoulders with their night leave requirements wrapped up in them, those being the days before the issue of brown cardboard attaché cases – he considered bundle men to have several screws loose. Wives cost money and a matlow hadn't much of that, not on two bob a day plus various allowances, pittances reckoned in pennies. Pay for a wife, make her out an allotment note, and there was sod-all left for *other* women or for booze. No use going to sea under those conditions. Leading Seaman Slugg liked variety in women and, oddly perhaps since he was no oil painting, hadn't found it hard to acquire them, for all the nice girls love a sailor.

Nice?

Well, that depended on your outlook. Slugg thought them nice. Maisie at the Golden Fleece, Vera at the Admiral Vernon, Doris at the Coal Exchange and a few others over the years, the total number boosted by Slugg's sojourn in the harbour-bound *Castile*. Good months, all things considered – filling in time for his pension. Then the war had broken out, the *Castile* had been dug out from reserve and made ready for sea service, and Slugg, barely out of the Andrew, had been recalled and drafted ultimately to the *Ark Royal*, from which he had been a survivor – there had been only one man lost in fact – when she went down in the Western Mediterranean. Slugg had

49

basked in a little glory on return to Pompey barracks and there had been more women but not much time to enjoy them, thanks to the war and the Drafting Jaunty in RNB who seemed intent upon sending seamen to sea.

Slugg came back to the present. 'Right,' he said. 'Cast off, lad. Back to the ship and get our 'eads down till the next pipe.'

ii

Next forenoon, now with little wind but with the snow drifting to whiten both ship and land, the *Castile* weighed anchor and pointed her bows for the floating dock, a massive chunk of concrete now low in the water, flooded to receive the light cruiser. She nudged in, carefully conned by Cameron from the forebridge, with the First Lieutenant in the eyes of the ship, Lieutenant Blake aft, Mr Marty amidships, all with their parties of seamen to tend wires as the ship was worked slowly in, the wires being passed for'ard by stages to be secured to the various sets of bollards on the sides of the floating dock. When the ship was in position the shoring beams were rigged under the supervision of the dock foreman and then wedged down hard with the sledgehammers. As soon as this had been done the dock began to lift and the water cascaded from the after end. When the ship was clear of the water with her bottom-plating resting on the central supports and the shoring beams holding her upright, tragedy struck. A rating put his foot in a bight of rope being worked on the quarterdeck, lost his balance as the jerk came on, and pitched head first over the side to land with a crump in the floor of the dock, taking the rope with him. The dockyard mateys carrying out an inspection below rushed to his assistance; when the surgeon lieutenant reached him, he was dead.

'Poor bloke' Mr Marty said. 'Just a kid.'

'And cack-handed with it,' Leading Seaman Pafford said

unfeelingly. Proper seaman didn't put their big plates of meat into bights of rope, not unless they meant to commit suicide when the rope moved.

On the bridge, Cameron grieved. Ordinary Seaman Rank had been nineteen years of age, a volunteer before his call-up, only just out of the *Royal Arthur* at Skegness, his first draft to sea. Cameron took the first opportunity of looking at the young seaman's parchment: only child and mother a widow. It was going to be a hard job to write to her. That was always a harrowing business for a commanding officer. On a lesser note, there would have to be an enquiry – simple enough, perhaps, but Admiralty bullshit always managed to make more of it than necessary and there was much else to do before the *Castile* left Scapa.

It was Mr Marty who put many of the ship's company's thoughts into words. 'Omen,' he said. 'In the circumstances, whatever *they* are. Don't like it, I don't.'

iii

The work was begun without delay. Heavy girders were brought aboard along with welding equipment and the fore messdecks were cleared of all hands and their clutter – hammocks and such personal gear as couldn't be crammed into the lockers. The mess tables were dismantled and removed as were the usual mess traps – bread barges, eating utensils, spitkids and so on. The spaces were bared to the bone and the dockyard mateys took over, the normal inhabitants, seamen and stokers, doing a good deal of moaning about it: they were to be accommodated temporarily aboard the *Iron Duke*, which would mean a lot of boat ferrying between the dock and the old battleship, and during working hours they would be as it were deprived of their home and nowhere to go for stand easy and a smoke other than someone else's mess. That first day in the floating dock there was little for the ship's company to do: no point even in attempting to keep the ship clean when dockyard mateys were aboard with all their muck and clutter.

'Make-and-mend, sir?' Brown suggested to Cameron.

Cameron nodded his agreement: a make-and-mend, at one time a period when the lower deck carried out essential repairs to their clothing, darning and so on, was now just the navy's term for a half holiday. At dinner time, after the spirit issue, Up Spirits having been supervised to the RPO's satisfaction by Mr Marty, the bosun's mate made the pipe over the Tannoy: 'Do you hear there . . . hands to make and mend clothes, stand fast the duty hands. 1st and 2nd motor cutters will leave the ship with libertymen at 1400 and 1500. All leave expires at 2200 tonight.'

Leading Seaman Pafford was in charge of the duty hands, the men always immediately available from the duty part of the watch aboard, the ones who got first call when there was an emergency or when any work was needed to be done out of routine. Kept aboard, Pafford went down to the seamen's messdeck and hung around the watertight door from the flat outside. Talk about work: the ship looked as if it was being rebuilt. He buttonholed one of the dockyard mateys.

'What's going on, eh?'

'Strengthening the bow section, mate.'

'What for?'

The man grinned and winked. 'Those that ask no questions, they don't get told no lies, right?'

'Not that you know sod all anyway,' Pafford said in disgust.'

'No. But I reckon you're due to hit something pretty hard.' The man went through to the messdeck, where there was a good deal of noise, banging of sledgehammers, and white glare from the welding torches. Pafford sucked in his cheeks: a ramming job? For what purpose? Convoy escort, like most of the navy, acting as a submarine smasher, ramming anything that surfaced?

Not particularly likely, that. Except that the officers

52

sitting on their arses in the Admiralty were quite capable of thinking up something just as daft. Pafford went back to the upper deck, where also things were happening and being watched by Chief Petty Officer Froggett.

'What's it all in aid of, buff?'

Froggett shrugged. 'Wish I knew. Skipper'll tell us when he's ready.'

'Maybe. And maybe not. Some do, some don't. Some think, where ignorance is bliss. . . .'

'Something to be said for that an' all.' Froggett pushed his cap back from his forehead, scratched and sighed. They looked like buggering up the poor old boat no end, the dockyard foremen had that sort of look in their eyes, speculative, as they poked and measured and made chalk marks all over Froggett's paintwork, right the way along the upper deck, superstructure and all. Next day there was no doubt about it, the ship was being strengthened, given extra armour along all exposed positions. The forebridge began to look like one of the old forts at Spithead, sticking out of the hogwash like dragon's teeth. Now even the buzzes were subdued: no invention could begin to cope, it seemed. Oddly, it was Ordinary Seaman Quentin who got there, spot on.

He gave his view to the chief gunner's mate, Bullshit Shine.

'*Vindictive*, GI,' he said, using the abbreviation for gunnery instructor, a chief gunner's mate's alternative title.

'*Vindictive*?'

'Not the present one. The last one of the name.'

Bullshit Shine stared. 'Zeebrugge, 1918?'

'That's it, GI. Blockship.'

'Well, I never. Bloody daft! This isn't the last lot, son. You don't have blockships now. Get blown out o' the bloody water on sight. Or before – picked up by the shore radar.' Shine looked around the decks, pursed his lips and shook his head. Then he said warningly. 'Look, sonny boy.

Just suppose you're right after all. Got there kind of accidental. Remember the posters: Be Like Dad, Keep Mum. Right? You'll get keelhauled else – so watch it.'

5

ORDINARY SEAMAN MacTavish managed to get blind drunk ashore: although the ration in the canteen was supposed to be two pints per man, there were always ways round that for a determined Scot. Also, MacTavish encountered an old mate from Glasgow, a friend he hadn't seen since early in the war. This man had illegally bottled several days' tots of grog and was willing to share.

For a while the two of them roared out Scots songs and naval ditties of the ruder sort. Then they lurched out from the canteen and made their way along a stony track with snow drifts piled at the sides. They were looking for women, somewhat fruitlessly since Scapa Flow was not Sauchiehall Street. The cold was bitter but the drink kept them warm, to start with anyway.

'Bloody place,' MacTavish said after a while.

'Sure to be women somewhere. What do the inhabitants do at night?'

'Sheep, I reckon,' MacTavish said.

'Aye . . . there was a story about a leading hand from the *Rodney* – ' MacTavish's companion broke off suddenly. 'Someone ahead there.' The snow had started falling again, and outlines were blurred.

'Aye, there is. But it's no' a woman.' It wasn't; it was the naval patrol, four seamen marching in files with a PO in charge. MacTavish, the drink catching up with him – the

55

contrast between the warmth of the canteen and the outside cold – staggered, lost his balance and fell flat in a flurry of snow.

The patrol came up and were halted by the PO. 'What's all this, then?'

'Sod off.'

The PO sighed: this was not entirely unusual for Scapa. 'On your feet, lad.'

MacTavish said nothing but struggled to his feet and swung a fist wildly at the petty officer, who dodged easily enough. A moment later MacTavish was in the hard grip of the patrol and being frogmarched away to the picquet house. His mate, not himself apprehended, tagged along behind. At the picquet house MacTavish, by now beginning to lose his speech, was brought before the officer of the patrol, a lieutenant RN.

'What ship?'

There was a mumble from MacTavish. His mate said, '*Castile*, sir.'

'A friend of yours?'

'Aye, sir. But I'm not a *Castile*, sir. *Iron Duke*, waiting for – '

'Yes, all right.' The lieutenant gave MacTavish a long-suffering look, then spoke to the petty officer. 'He'll have to be returned to his ship, PO. *Castile* is – ' He broke off from an indiscretion. 'We'll leave it to them to charge him. Put him in the guard room until the first of *Castile*'s libertyboats comes in, then send him off – with an escort if necessary.'

When MacTavish arrived back aboard to be charged by the Officer of the Watch, who had no option considering MacTavish's condition, he was observed by the chief gunner's mate. Bullshit Shine didn't, of course, carry out his earlier threat of physical violence: the navy didn't work like that. But he would remember, for what that might be worth now. What *did* the future hold? Quentin's words had made a kind of sense despite what Shine had said in return.

56

Quentin had eyes and a brain – he was a candidate for an RNVR commission, after all. And if Quentin should be proved right, then why harass an OD for getting himself as pissed as a newt for perhaps the very last time in his life?

ii

The work went on throughout the next five days, the dockyard mateys working through the nights under the glare of yardarm groups. Cameron had never known dockyard mateys keep at it for so long at a stretch. Down in the dockyards of the south, or the civilian shipyards on the Clyde, work was stopped more often, he had sometimes thought, than it was on. Tea breaks, card-playing, strikes too, demarcation disputes in the middle of a war as to who painted what, who shifted what, who undid certain screws.

But not now. Presumably there was a financial inducement behind the almost feverish activity, a bonus if the work was done on time. That didn't ever apply to the officers and men who had to sail the ships and take them into action. You lived hard – very hard, along the messdecks – fought and died, all for your statutory pay and no more. No overtime, no bonuses for a spot-on arrival at the scene of action. Get killed and you were just written off the Admiralty's books and that was that. . . .

Cameron, who was currently taking a mental break from paper work and letting his thoughts run free, caught himself up. It did no good to think along those lines. There was a war to be fought and never mind the lack of financial rewards . . . but somehow, that day beneath the northern snowfall, he had found himself unable to concentrate on routine paper work, reports on this, that and the other, signing of documents relating to his ship's company, oil fuel consumption, stores lists – the *Castile* was carrying no paymaster, so that burden largely fell on the Captain along with all the other burdens, and a ship had to be stored no matter what her mission. Right to the bitter end the bumph had to reign supreme. There were certain departments in the offices of the various Commanders-in-Chief and at the Admiralty itself that considered the proper presentation of lists in due time as of more importance than the accurate firing of the guns. If a salvo missed its target, it missed; but woe betide you if you failed to account properly for a tin of herrings-in-tomato-sauce, the navy's mealtime stand-by, known to the lower deck either simply as herrings-in or as red lead.

Now there was Ordinary Seaman MacTavish, placed by the Officer of the Watch, Lieutenant Blake, in the First Lieutenant's Report and, because MacTavish had been belligerent to Brown at Defaulters, forwarded on to Captain's Report. Any minute now: Cameron glanced at the brassbound clock on the bulkhead behind his roll-top desk. With three minutes to go, Lieutenant Brown knocked at the cabin door and entered with his cap beneath his left arm.

'Captain's Defaulters, sir. All present and correct.'

'All right, Number One.' Cameron screwed the cap back on his fountain pen and stood up. He left his cabin followed by the First Lieutenant and strode the short distance to the after end of the flat where the criminals were lined up under the eye of the Regulating Petty Officer and the various witnesses to wrong-doing who would be called upon to give evidence. There were four men in all. Their crimes: slow in obeying a pipe for the duty hands, Leading Seaman Pafford prosecuting; failed to attend the muster when Both Watches for Exercise had been piped, presented by the chief bosun's mate; answering back to the chief stoker. Cameron, wondering what the point of it all was when their small world was due to erupt, gave them a pep-talk about discipline and then merely cautioned them and they were wheeled away out of it to carry on with their duties.

Then the bad lad, ordered like the others to remove his cap in the presence of the Captain at the Defaulters' Table.

'Ordinary Seaman MacTavish, sir, Official Number P/JX

58

187153. Did return aboard in a state of intoxication, sir.'
The RPO, ship's policeman, cleared his throat. 'And was
subsequently abusive to the First Lieutenant, sir, using the
words, away and bugger off you stupid sod, sir.'

Cameron suppressed a grin: the words, formally uttered,
failed to fit with the solemnity of the occasion and the
pomposity of the RPO's tone. He glanced first at Blake,
interrogatively.

'Mr Blake, you were the Officer of the Watch?'

'Yes, sir.' Blake stepped forward and saluted. He gave
the facts of a boozy arrival aboard.

'Have you anything to say, MacTavish?'

'Aye, sir. Och, I was pissed – drunk – right enough, sir.
I'm sorry, sir. I didna do any damage, sir.'

'No, I accept that, but it's scarcely the point, is it?'

MacTavish didn't answer.

The RPO said, 'Answer the Captain.'

'Och, away an' get stuffed, ye daft prat.'

The RPO's mouth opened, fishlike. Cameron met
Brown's eye. A fresh crime had now been committed and
the matter was becoming involved, but it was a way out of a
sort, a deferment of decision being appropriate and proper.
'Remanded,' Cameron said abruptly.

'Remanded,' the RPO echoed. 'On cap. Salute the
Captain. About turn. Double march.'

MacTavish went away at an ungainly trot: you couldn't
really double in such an enclosed space, Cameron thought,
but of course the routine had to be observed. He caught the
eye of the RPO, who was looking huffy. 'Don't take it to
heart, Petty Officer Parker.'

'I'll not do that, sir.' The police face split into a cautious
grin. 'Been called worse, sir.'

'I'm sorry to hear that,' Cameron said gravely. 'All right,
Number One, carry on, please.'

The officers and witnesses saluted and dispersed about
their various duties. Before going back to his paper work,
Cameron climbed to the forebridge. Some hefty work had

59

been done, thick protective sheeting reaching above the glass screen. It looked effective but gunfire could make short enough work of it, heavy gunfire anyway. Cameron looked away across the grey water towards the shore and its lying snow, the hutted buildings of the base covered except where the coal-fed stoves had thawed the roofs and chimneys. Cameron shivered: what a dump! How could you blame a man for getting himself blotto? Better that than go round the bend. But you couldn't excuse abuse of an officer or petty officer, you could never allow discipline to suffer – a concept for the good of all hands and the ship. If Ordinary Seaman MacTavish happened to come through the next few days, he would have to be dealt with. Meanwhile, he had it all hanging over his head and would still have it in action. So, for that matter, would Cameron. Another of a captain's worries, and Cameron took his duty seriously. Discipline and justice – the two had to marry up. When they didn't, you could get a disaffected ship's company, very quickly.

The wind was getting up now, and the sky was as bleak as the sea. Beyond the headlands the water was ruffling into white horses. The dry dock, well moored, was safe against dragging; the wind was still being deflected by the configuration of the land. But once they were away to sea. . . . Cameron had studied the weather projections and they would be in for a blow, but that was all to the good. In fair weather you stood out more, and the mission would in any case have waited for the right conditions.

iii

Peter Blake, lieutenant RNVR, made the rounds of his guns with Mr Marty and the chief gunner's mate, together with the leading hand of the gunner's party – the Marty Party as it had now inevitably become known. Blake had by now been taken into Cameron's confidence and he knew that the guns were going to be all important in getting the

Castile to her objective, after which they would largely lose
their importance except possibly as back-up. Blake was not
entirely happy professionally: his knowledge of gunnery
was limited to a short, very short, course at Whale Island,
nothing that began to approach the Long G course, two
years of it, that a peacetime RN lieutenant was required to
undergo before he could call himself a specialist gunnery
officer. Blake knew that the kingpin aboard *Castile* was in
fact Mr Marty, gunner RN; and after him, Bullshit Shine.
The leading hand of the Marty Party was Leading Seaman
Slugg: the ship being in reduced complement he was
doubling his duties as such – his job was to supervise the
gunner's store and keep a check on the ammunition supply
– with those of motor-cutter's coxswain.

Blake saw that CPO Shine was wearing a sardonic look
while they made their rounds. 'Been a gunnery officer long,
sir, have you?'

'I was second GO in the *Cumberland*, Chief.'

'Oh-ah.' Shine blew out his cheeks and tapped them,
making a sound like a tom-tom. Mr Marty, who knew that
this meant 'I don't bloody well believe it but I suppose I
must' gave the GI a discreet nudge.

Mr Marty said reflectively, '*Cumberland*, eh. Eight-inch
. . . and more guns than what we've been left with. Good
old tubs, the County Class, but buggers in a seaway – right,
Mr Blake?'

'Dead right, Guns. Too much freeboard. Roll your guts
out.'

'And sod up the gunlayers.'

They moved on, a small procession intent on checking
every detail. Chief Petty Officer Shine had an eagle eye
when it came to detail and Leading Seaman Slugg had a
note pad and pencil ready, writing it all down to Shine's
dictation. One of Shine's enemies was dirt – dirt in the guns
or the gun's-crews. Rust was a sin before God. All moving
parts must be kept greased.

'Leading Seaman Slugg?'

61

Slugg moved faster than normal, for the tone had been harsh. 'Yes, GI?'

'Paintwork – see it?'

A small scratch. 'Yes, GI. I'll – '

'Them dockyard mateys I'll be bound, filthy buggers.' Bullshit Shine rose and fell on the balls of his feet, hands clasped behind the back of his Number Three uniform, the working one with red badges in place of gold. 'Scratches, Leading Seaman Slugg, lets in the wet and what do you get, eh? Rust. First thing you know, the whole bloody gun falls off its mounting. Right?'

Slugg sucked at his teeth. All gunner's mates exaggerated, it was part of their make-up. 'Yes, GI.'

'See the Captain of the gun's given a charge of dynamite up his arse – soon as Mr Blake's satisfied, that is.'

Lieutenant Blake wondered how he was to manifest satisfaction to the satisfaction of the GI. The guns had all looked perfectly all right to him; and he happened to know, now, that patches of rust would stand scant chance of developing aboard the *Castile*. But he couldn't put that point to Chief PO Shine, who would only look at him in wonderment if he did. Thinking, so what? To Shine, the future would be the future and could be relied upon to bring its own problems. Currently a scratch was a scratch, and heinous.

Blake, thinking his own thoughts which were largely of home, for he had recently got himself married, caught his foot against a bollard and stumbled. He would have gone flat on his face had not Shine grabbed him.

'All right, sir, are you?'

'Yes, thank you, GI.' Blake was embarrassed, flustered. A stumble was not good for one's dignity aboard a ship.

'Want to watch where you put your feet, sir. That rating. . . .'

'Yes.'

'It's a long way to the dock bottom, sir.'

Blake thought: why the hell can't he leave it? He knew

Shine thought he was a bit wet behind the ears: Shine had that expressive face. Blake's principal wish was that the bloody war was over and he was back in the West Country – Bodmin, with the wildness of the moor handy for week-end walks when the weather permitted. Estate agency work could be dull, but at least it was safe and clear-cut and he liked going home each night much more than he liked standing a watch on the bridge in gales and rain, buffetted and half frozen and drinking cup after cup of thick cocoa brought up by the bridge messenger to keep a flicker of warmth going. He wondered, as he walked ahead of Mr Marty and tried to watch his feet as well as the guns, what Mary Anne would be doing. Probably not much in fact, since she was living with her parents – they'd not been able to find a home of their own yet and it was cheaper to live with in-laws though this would have its restrictions when he was on leave next time – if there was ever to be a next time: Peter Blake suddenly remembered again. But you had to look on the bright side and look forward to leave and its pleasures. Perhaps they'd stay somewhere, the small hotel in Looe where they'd spent the brief honeymoon, a friendly place and they could be all by themselves again. Mr and Mrs Larkspur, Mary Anne's parents, were very nice but the bungalow was very small, just the two bedrooms divided by a partition and the Larkspurs had their bed right up alongside the partition, while their own was slap bang against it the other side, which showed a lack of imagination. Blake had suggested they moved it but Mary Anne hadn't wanted to, mum would be upset and would wonder. As it happened Mr Larkspur was a loud and continual snorer, so that helped up to a point; they'd had to wait until the snoring started, but that wasn't satisfactory either, since the regularity of the snores had caused Peter Blake to count them which had taken his mind off more urgent matters and there had been accusations that he didn't love Mary Anne.

Life wasn't really and truly all that good on the home

front: Blake blamed the war for that. It would all be fine once the war was over and they were together all the time. Or would it? There were nagging doubts. Mary Anne was a pouter and in quite a short time he had come to dread the next protrusion of lips. At first it had been attractive, but the attraction had waned. . . .

'Mr Blake?'

Blake came back to the *Castile*. 'Yes, Guns?'

'Asked if you'd seen enough.'

'Sorry, Guns. Yes – yes, I have. It all seems pretty good. Well done, GI.'

Bullshit Shine just stared. Blake turned away and went down to the wardroom. Stand Easy had just been piped. As he went he heard Shine's voice: '*Cumberland*, eh. Not one of the old *Castiles*. Not one of *us*, like. We're special.'

Mr Marty said, 'Maybe we are. But better not to think like that. We're all one ship's company now. With a job to do, what's more.'

'And what's the job, sir?'

'Wait for the skipper,' Mr Marty said.

Shine went below to the petty officers' mess, where he lit a Players and blew smoke that joined with that from all the other fags to form a blue haze across the lockers. What a man would do without a fag . . . it was a sort of panacea that put the frustrations of life in their place, something to look forward to after fagless hours on the upper deck at night, after action, after watching a greenhorn make out he knew what the guns were for. Like Blake, Chief PO Shine often thought of home and Rosie all alone in the flat in Rowlands Castle, except for the landlord and his wife who lived in the bottom flat. They didn't fraternize much. The landlord and his wife were in their eighties and kept themselves to themselves. Shine thought about home mostly during such periods of Stand Easy, and at night in his hammock: unlike Blake, he was able to put Rosie in the background when he was on duty – years of sea experience, of long absences, had taught him how to do that. If you wanted to get on, you had to separate things out.

Home thoughts today were cut into by Chief Stoker Rump.

'Any buzzes, GI?'

'Course not. Where'd I pick up buzzes, may I ask?'

'Marty.'

'Sealed lips. *If* he knows any more'n we do.'

'What do you reckon, then?'

'I don't. No use speculating, Rumpo.' Shine wasn't going to repeat Ordinary Seaman Quentin's prognostication, right or wrong. He changed the subject. 'What's your lot like, down below?'

'Mixture. Largely HO. Some good 'ands though. That's another thing.'

'What is?'

'Full stokehold complement. The only department that's up to normal strength. Except it's just Rogers in charge, no commander(E) or even a two-and-a -half. But the stokers and tiffies – like I said, full muster. I'm wondering why – that's all.'

Shine ejected a fragment of tobacco from his mouth. 'Means your bloody engines are going to be important for once.'

'They always are and you know it, GI. But I'm still left wondering. Why – this time – the engines above all? What it says to me is . . . I reckon the old ship's going to need to be kept going even when – '

'Even when all the rest has stopped, eh?'

Rump nodded. 'Something like that. To the bitter bleeding end.'

'Could be right,' Shine said non-committally. The chief stoker was about to say something else when the Tannoy came on, the bosun's mate blew a blast on his bosun's call and passed the order for Out Pipes. Stand Easy at an end, the ship's company drifted back to its daily routine. Later that morning the Fleet Post Office delivered the mail aboard and soon after this Cameron was ordered by signal to repair aboard the *Iron Duke* forthwith. He obeyed his order with half his mind elsewhere. One of his letters had been from home in Aberdeen. His mother wrote that his father had been knocked down by a lorry, reversing in the docks. He was in hospital and not too good – there had been concussion, and although he had come round fairly quickly he was being kept in bed. Reading between the lines Cameron believed his mother was more than normally anxious and would have liked him to ask for compassionate leave but had almost certainly been prevented from the direct appeal by his father, who would very likely be furious that she'd written at all.

In any case compassionate leave would be out of the question and was even more so after Cameron's visit to the *Iron Duke*: fresh orders had been received from the Admiralty. The *Castile* was to be in all respects ready for sea forty-eight hours earlier than originally scheduled and a chance was to be taken on the weather: reports had come in via Intelligence of certain German troop movements. Dynamite, figuratively, would be placed beneath the dockyard mateys to get the structural work advanced.

On his return to his ship, Cameron was met at the head of the accommodation ladder by the First Lieutenant in addition to the Officer of the Watch and the usual gangway staff.

'All well, Number One?'

'Yes, sir – '

'Good! You have a worried look.'

'Nothing to bother about, sir.'

'All right, Number One. I'd like a word with you.'

Cameron turned away and, followed by Brown, made for his cabin in the stern of the ship. His steward was waiting, flicking a duster over the mahogany woodwork. 'Gin, please, Weem.'

'Aye, aye, sir.' Leading Steward Weem left the day cabin for his pantry. He was quickly back with his tray, a bottle of Gordon's gin, a jug of water, two glasses and a small bottle of bitters. At Cameron's nod he poured two small tots and once again left the cabin, keeping his ears a-cock bill for titbits of news. Cameron, who knew the facts of sea life well enough, kept his voice low as he recounted the fresh orders.

'We'll have our work cut out, sir,' Brown said. 'Or the dockyard mateys will.'

'Chase 'em hard, Number One. If we're not ready we'll leave just the same. If we don't, we're going to be jumped on from a very great height.'

'We'll be ready,' Brown said. 'What about the Marines?'

'Rescheduled, same as us. Embarkation from a destroyer, rendezvousing off Lamlash in the Clyde. Under cover of darkness.' Cameron looked sideways at Brown: there was worry there, all right, a pre-occupation, and it wasn't to do with the ship or Brown would have come out with it. 'Another gin, Number One?'

'Better not, sir, thank you.'

'That had a reluctant sound. It won't do you any harm. If there's anything up – why not tell me?' Cameron had good personal reason for knowing the mail had come aboard; so often in wartime the mail was a two-edged sword for men about to go to sea.

'It's all right,' Brown said rather edgily. It was personal, right enough. Cameron just nodded and poured the gin. Two and two could be put together and made to add up to a woman. Most troubles were women, and Brown was married. . . .

Cameron said, 'Bottoms up, Number One.'

'Bottoms up, sir.' They downed the gins in a swallow apiece and Brown excused himself to go about his duties. Cameron watched him leave, saw again the look of dejection. He wished he could have helped; but Brown was a good few years older than himself and wouldn't appreciate advice if this did happen to be a matrimonial situation and Cameron fancied it could well be: John Brown had already mentioned that his wife ran a club for officers in Portsmouth and having said that he'd turned the conversation somewhat quickly as though he'd uttered an indiscretion or had seemed to offer an implied criticism. Officers' clubs in wartime were something of a risk for husbands away at sea. For wives too, come to that. Cameron shrugged: it wasn't his concern except insofar as he might now have a second-in-command with his mind on other matters. And there was nothing to be done about that at this stage.

iv

Brown stood in his cabin, fists clenched, staring out through his port at the barrenness of Scapa Flow but seeing only his wife and the home in Fareham. Who did you believe? In Brown's view the writers of anonymous letters were the scum of the earth but where there was smoke, he had always believed, there was likely to be fire. Anyway, he'd had his own doubts. The writer of the letter – it was typed, so there was no indication as to whether it came from a man or a woman though he suspected it was more likely to be the latter – thought he ought to know. Why? Wasn't it far better to be in ignorance when there was nothing you could do about it currently? But no: *he ought to know* . . . ought to know that different naval and army officers had been seen over the last few months, coming and going. Like a brothel, the letter writer said unctuously. Truth or jealousy? John Brown knew there were women in Fareham and in Pompey who wouldn't have been averse to hopping into bed with him, but he'd never been interested and had never given any encouragement.

The letter was now crumpled in a fist. He released the fist and tore the letter, viciously, into shreds, then burned them in an ashtray with the flame of his lighter. The dirty bastard – dirty bitch! He wasn't going to believe any of it, he told himself, but not with very much conviction since he had those memories of leaves when he'd been left on his own all day. That was what rankled now. He was broadminded enough to know and accept that women as well as men had sexual feelings and to be deprived for long periods of a husband . . . but to think that perhaps when he'd been on leave she'd preferred someone else – that hit hard. Though of course he could be entirely wrong. He wished he had a revolver, and the opportunity to go south and sort someone out before the *Castile* sailed and never came back. But perhaps he would never need to worry. Perhaps that would be just as well.

He took a grip, left his cabin and sent for the lieutenant(E) and the chief bosun's mate to begin the process of chasing the dockyard mateys to cut forty-eight hours off their completion time.

6

'ADDRESSED Lieutenant-Commander Cameron, sir,' a paymaster lieutenant said. He had a naval message form in his hand and was speaking to the Duty Captain in the Admiralty's Operations Room. 'The Scapa base has had orders in regard to the *Castile* – orders to intercept any last-minute telegrams . . . the original telegram was addressed c/o GPO London, sir, delivered to FMO Scapa, who opened it and contacted us for orders.'

'Well? What does it say?'

The paymaster lieutenant handed the message form to the Duty Captain. The telegram had been from Cameron's mother: his father had had a stroke and had unexpectedly died. 'I'm very sorry,' the Captain said. 'Very sorry indeed. Damn rotten luck.'

'Yes, sir. What do we do?'

'Hold it,' the Captain said briefly. 'Not the time to worry a commanding officer with news of this sort.'

'Compassionate leave, sir –'

'For God's sake grow up,' the Captain said irritably. His face red, the paymaster lieutenant gathered up a sheaf of papers and left the Operations Room. The *Castile* . . . possibly Cameron would never know in any case, not in this world. One could only be sorry for the mother in Aberdeen. Back in his own office, the paymaster lieutenant drafted a signal for the Fleet Mail Officer at Scapa,

70

repeating the Duty Captain's order. Nothing was to disturb the *Castile*'s mission, or her Captain's peace of mind.

ii

There had been mail also for Yeoman of Signals Robbins: another death. The death reported to Robbins was that of his sister-in-law's husband, a relative of a sort but not close. Not cancer after all: an ulcer had burst and he'd gone. Robbins was sorry, of course, mainly for the boys and Dorothy, but it did open up horizons. Not that he'd ever fancied his sister-in-law, but he'd known her as long as he'd known Dorothy and single life was a lonely business and one day the war would end and he would be back to shore life. Mind, there were the laws of consanguinity and Robbins wasn't sure whether or not a deceased wife's sister was out of bounds when it came to matrimony. However, it was something to think about for the future.

On the flag deck, Robbins cast an eye around his flag locker, checking on his leading signalman: all in order by the look of it, the various flags neatly stowed and the clips ready for bending onto the signal halliards in double quick time. As he made a visual check of the big signalling projector, Chief PO Froggett came up the ladder.

'Morning, Yeo.'

'Morning, buff. If you can call it that.' The sky was grey as ever and the wind, though it had moderated somewhat, was cold.

'Lousy dump,' Froggett said. 'Not for much longer, though, I reckon.'

'Eh?'

'Shore leave's cancelled,' Froggett said briefly. 'Read into that what you like. It'll be piped later.' He went on towards the forebridge, leaving Robbins to guess at the facts, which probably were that the *Castile* was under sailing orders. Later as forecast by Froggett the pipe was made by the bosun's mate of the afternoon watch: all liberty was

71

cancelled and the ship would undock at first light next day. In the meantime a naval cock-up was being made in the Fleet Mail Office, where an elderly three-badge able seaman, long past his prime, was discovering an undelivered and opened telegram addressed to Lieutenant-Commander Cameron aboard the *Castile*. Bad news: the AB pursed his lips. Poor bloke, the ship about to sail by all accounts or buzzes . . . he stuck down the flap of the buff-coloured envelope and put it in the tray for delivery to the drifter that acted as tender to ships in the floating dock. By means of another naval cock-up the drifter developed engine trouble and her routine calls were cancelled soon after the telegram and other recently delivered matter had been put aboard. Her troubles were cured during the night and she was standing off just as the *Castile* was moving astern out of the floating dock.

The drifter skipper spoke to the light cruiser through his megaphone.

'*Castile* ahoy! There's a delivery for you.'

Lieutenant Brown shouted back. 'Follow us to the destroyer anchorage, come alongside once we're anchored.'

'Aye. . . .'

On the bridge Cameron checked his sternway and put the engines ahead. With the cable and side party standing by on the fo'c'sle, and Brown now in the eyes of the ship with his anchor flags, the *Castile* moved at slow speed to be brought up off the naval base. When his transit bearings began to come on, Cameron lifted his own anchor flag. Brown did likewise; and when the flags came down sharply and the verbal order was passed from the bridge to let go, the starboard anchor cable went out in a flurry of rust and a loud clatter as it leapt around the cable-holder. Brown checked the outrush with the third shackle on deck and as soon as the ship had got her cable the drifter came alongside and a canvas bag was put aboard.

iii

Cameron's initial and natural instinct was to get to

Aberdeen as fast as possible: his mother would need him now, and to hell with the war. He poured a stiff gin, his fingers shaking so that some of it went over the side of the glass. The gin helped to steady him. He had his duty to do and it was too late even to consider, seriously, asking for a relief CO. With the ship under sailing orders and all leave cancelled, it wouldn't do for the Captain to go ashore even to telephone. He had to go through with it and he knew very well that that was what his father would have said. Captain Cameron would never want anyone to duck his duty, to back out and leave a mission like a bird with a broken wing, deprived of the captain at the last moment, left with a hurriedly appointed substitute who would have to get to know the ship and her company all over again, a real pier-head jump.

And his father had served in the old *Castile*, had been full of pride on getting the news that his son was to command her. Cameron remembered his words clearly: 'Be worthy of it – right? She's a good ship. Look after her for me. Treat her well. Bring her through – whatever's to come.'

That, he would do. More than ever now. It had all become even more personal.

Cameron looked at the gin bottle. No more: once started, it might not stop. His mind went back into the past, the old peacetime days when he'd been a child and a youth, going aboard his father's ship, a deep-sea cargo liner . . . the thrill of being the Master's son, of seeing the deference of officers and men, the knowledge that his father took the ship to all parts of the world, through all the seven seas, through storm and tempest, calm and brilliant tropic sun, picking up his landfalls spot-on after sometimes weeks at sea across endless oceans. Days when his father had been on leave and himself home from school and they had been a complete family for a brief spell and, for a while at least, his father had become less remote, less godlike. Once, he had remarked on that.

'You're different when you've been home a bit, Daddy.'

'Oh? In what way?' Captain Cameron had raised his eyebrows, smiling.

'I – I don't really know. Closer . . . not so formal.'

'I suppose you mean more relaxed. Well, that's true, of course. You can't entirely relax at sea. A captain's always on duty, Donald. Besides, there's another thing.' Captain Cameron had come out with something that the youngster was never to forget and was to see as absolute truth once he himself had gone to sea. 'The Captain has to keep apart. He can be friendly, but not too friendly. If he is, discipline suffers and he doesn't get – or deserve – the same respect. He has to be a lonely man most of the time, both in the merchant service and the navy.' Having said that, his father had given a laugh, ruffled his son's hair, and said, 'Common sense! Get too close and the men rumble you! We're not all perfect.'

Reverie was interrupted by the First Lieutenant, bringing reports: the ship would be ready on time. The dockyard mateys had only clearing-up work to do now mostly, with just a few more shoring beams to be set up in the fo'c'sle mess decks.

'Sandbags round the bridge, sir – ?'

'Not yet, Number One. After Lamlash – there'll be time then.'

'Yes, sir.'

'And hammocks once we're full away from Arran. Clear all nettings and have 'em brought up to all exposed positions.'

Brown grinned. 'Just like Nelson's navy! All round the upper deck of the *Victory*. I dare say you've been aboard, sir?'

Cameron nodded, felt a twinge. 'Yes. My father took me once.' No word about the loss: the ship's company mustn't know of personal grief; that could cause a loss of confidence as the *Castile* headed out for the enemy.

Brown left the cabin. Cameron went out soon after, to walk his decks, satisfy himself that all was as it should be.

74

He had brief words with individual ratings among his ship's company, words of confidence and authority. He spoke in particular to the old *Castile* hands, the men from those previous commissions, and noted the special feeling among them, the feeling of family, the determination that the old tub's happy image would be maintained. They all shared his own commitment: that in itself was, he found, immensely heartening.

Cameron climbed to the bridge at 0600 next morning, another grey and windswept day, and ordered the cable to be shortened-in for weighing. Once again the drifter came alongside and embarked the dockyard mateys, to take them to the *Iron Duke* where, on security grounds and to stifle careless talk where it might matter, they would remain for an indefinite period before being sent back to Portsmouth dockyard.

Cameron lifted a hand in acknowledgement as the First Lieutenant, on the fo'c'sle, reported the cable shortened-in. 'Weigh and hold it at the waterline, Number One,' he called down.

'Aye, aye, sir.' Until the ship was clear of the land's constrictions the anchor would remain held on the brake, ready for letting go in an emergency. Even before the flukes of the anchor had come into view, Cameron had passed the order that put his engines ahead and had given the first helm orders for Switha Sound and the exit into the Pentland Firth. Below in the engine-room, on the starting platform, Lieutenant(E) Rogers watched the repeater, heard the clang of the bells as the pointers moved in conformity with the telegraphs in the wheelhouse. The engine spaces began their vibration as the shafts turned for half speed ahead. Rogers was glad enough to leave Scapa: they all were. It was an inhospitable place, nothing to do ashore, no women as Ordinary Seaman MacTavish had discovered to his cost. Rogers, the proverbial seafaring womanizer, had felt the deprivation. Once away to sea you didn't think too much about it but when you were in port you expected a little

75

satisfaction. The recent mail delivery had brought news for Rogers: in his case not death but birth. Or so the writer of the letter feared. Rogers was worried: he wasn't the marrying sort and there had been hints in the letter that he might be expected to make an honest woman of the girl.

Chief ERA Hollyman, moving around and keeping an eye open on everything at once, had also had mail, a long letter from his wife, nothing of much importance in itself but it had brought a comforting glow to Hollyman's heart just to know the family was safe and well. That was all he asked, that Hitler should steer clear of them. As the *Castile* headed out to make westwards for Cape Wrath, Hollyman went into the boiler room for a word with Chief Stoker Rump.

'All right, Rumpo?'

'Right as it'll ever be. The old girl's not getting any younger. Would have been scrapped if it 'adn't bin for the war. Like all the C and D boats.' Rump wiped at his face with a ball of cotton-waste. 'I've got a feeling. . . .'

'What?'

'Never mind.'

'Go on. Don't keep me in bloody suspense, eh?'

Rump said, 'I reckon she's not due to come back from this lot.'

'You could say the same of any ship in wartime,' Hollyman said, and went back to his engine-room. Sod Rumpo, saying a thing like that, just now of all times. The trouble was, he himself felt it too. He believed a lot of the old hands did; you could see it now and again in their faces, in the withdrawn expressions that flitted now and again. Just a seaman's nature, of course; they were a superstitious bunch. You didn't whistle at sea, you didn't like corpses or parsons aboard, you didn't kill albatrosses, you knew that each shitehawk, or seagull to a landlubber, that dropped its load on the decks sheltered the roving soul of a mariner dead and gone. You knew all that, and you had a funny feeling when you saw so many other faces from the past,

76

men who had sailed in the old *Castile* before. And they still didn't know what they were in for, this time.

But the skipper would probably tell them before long. Or would he? None of them really knew Cameron yet. He could be a stuffy bugger but Hollyman didn't believe he was. He was RNVR and he was young, not yet fossilized into RN ways . . . Chief ERA Hollyman had a peacetime memory of a mentally constipated captain RN hovering on the brink of the retired list who had taken the secrecy angle of a combined fleet exercise so much to heart that he had fooled even his commander(E), with the result that the ship had run out of oil fuel in the middle of the Mediterranean and had had to be taken in tow to Malta.

iv

'Stop engines.'

'Stop engines, sir.' Lieutenant Batten repeated the order down the voicepipe to Chief PO Barker, who as chief quartermaster was on the wheel for the arrival off Arran in the Firth of Clyde. Barker repeated it back and nodded at his telegraphsman, Ordinary Seaman Quentin, who pulled over the telegraph handles. The ship drifted with the wheel amidships.

It was full dark; on the bridge Cameron looked through his binoculars towards the great mass of Arran with the peak of Goat Fell rearing up behind the small settlement of Lamlash. There was some moon but a lot of cloud, so the light was fitful. Lamlash Bay, in the lee of Holy Island, appeared empty, so much Cameron was able to see as a streak of moonlight came down on the water.

'Blighters are adrift,' he remarked to Batten.

'Yes.' Batten also was using his binoculars, as were the lookouts in the bridge wings. Then a moment later he picked up some movement, something coming out from the direction of the pierhead at Lamlash, and he reported to the Captain.

'Right, Pilot, got them.' Cameron lowered his binoculars and walked to the after end of the bridge. He called down aft: 'Stand by, Number One. Coming off now.'

They waited, with all the way off the ship now, silent on a dark and silent sea, a silence that was scarcely broken by the few mutterings from the hands on deck, plus the odd nervy laugh as someone cracked a joke to relieve his tension. In the wheelhouse Chief PO Barker lit a fag, handed the packet to Quentin.

'Thanks, Chief.'

'Shouldn't really.'

'Why not, Chief?'

'Bad for you,' Barker said briefly, dragging in a deep lungful of smoke and blowing it out again. 'My old dad, he used to say, if I kept on smoking fags, I'd not be worth a kick on the arse by the time I was twenty-one. Mind, I've smoked ever since.'

'And you're still here, Chief.'

'Aye, that's right. Tell you something, lad. If your dad had ever kicked your arse, 'e'd 'ave ended up with a broken foot.' Barker chuckled. 'Don't you ever take any exercise? In for a commission an' all . . . they don't like fat officers, I reckon, not young ones anyway. I once –' He broke off; there had been a bump alongside, followed by a scraping noise. 'Here they come, perishin' bootnecks.'

'Bootnecks, Chief?'

'Royal Marines, sonny boy. Boots are leather. Back in Nelson's day they wore bloody great leather stocks round their necks. Collars, like 'orses.'

Quentin nodded. The buzz had spread that they were to embark a party of marines, probably commandos rather than the spit-and-polish marines who manned part of the main armament aboard the big ships of the fleet and provided the buglers and ceremonial bands; and in Quentin's view this reinforced his private theory about the approaching employment of the *Castile*. Now that the time for action seemed to be approaching, Quentin felt a stir of fear in his stomach. They wouldn't have far to go if his ideas proved right. By this time next day the ship could be a shambles. A few moments later he heard the shouted orders, followed by a tramp of many booted feet along the upper deck, and a rattle of arms and equipment.

Cameron was watching from the bridge as the commando party embarked: a major of marines, with a captain and two lieutenants, a colour sergeant, eight other NCOs, eighty men, all armed to the teeth with sub-machine guns, knives, grenades, lengths of fuse and case after case of ammunition. Each man was in camouflage uniform and with his face blackened with boot polish.

'Pretty murderous,' Batten remarked with a grin.

Shepherded by the chief bosun's mate and their own sergeants, the commandos went below. The major came up the ladder to the bridge, escorted by the First Lieutenant. Cameron saw a tall, vigorous-looking man with a thin, lined face cut in two by a heavy moustache.

'Wilson,' the major said, and reached out a hand.

'Cameron. Welcome aboard, Major. I hope you and your men'll be comfortable.'

'Well, it won't be for long anyhow.' The major lowered his voice. 'Do I take it all your chaps know the score – or not?'

'They will very soon. I'll pass the word as soon as we're away.' Cameron turned to the First Lieutenant. 'All correct, Number One?'

'Yes, sir. All boats cast off and going back inshore.'

'Right! Half ahead both engines, Pilot. Starboard ten.' The *Castile* came back to life, her plates shaking to the thrust of the screws, her head beginning to swing to starboard below Inchmarnock Water and the Cumbraes. As her bows swept round to point towards Troon on the Ayrshire coast, and then farther, Cameron steadied her for the outward passage past Ailsa Craig for the North Channel.

They slid down the Firth of Clyde, passing the landmarks

well remembered by so many of them from past commissions – Prestwick, Ayr and Turnberry to port, then between Ailsa Craig and Girvan for Corsewall Point outside Loch Ryan. As the *Castile* moved into the North Channel and set her course for the south, Cameron took up the microphone of the Tannoy and clicked the switch on.

'This is the Captain speaking,' he said. 'The ship is bound for the port of Dieppe in Occupied France.'

7

Now there was no need to ask about buzzes: they knew the score. Cameron had been explicit; as he said to the First Lieutenant and Major Wilson, who had remained on the bridge, he liked to keep his ship's company informed just as soon as he was able to release information.

'Right you were, son,' the chief gunner's mate said to Ordinary Seaman Quentin. The ship was now in two watches, four on and four off until they neared the French coast, and in a two-watch system Quentin was on Number Four gun aft, which would also be his action station when the ship was piped to first degree of readiness. 'Blockship, eh!'

'Yes, GI.' Quentin hesitated. 'What d'you rate our chances, GI?'

'Chances? What bloody chances? In the Andrew, son, you don't have *chances*. You goes in and bloody *wins*, all right?'

Quentin grinned. 'If you say so, GI.'

'I says so.' Chief PO Shine marched away, arms swinging. With a colour sergeant of marines aboard, there was a need to be extra smart, and never mind that no-one could see him in the dark. Bullshit Shine didn't rate the marines at all highly, not as compared with the naval gunnery branch, who were the king pins of the Senior Service. Marines were half soldiers, ruddy pongoes, brown jobs, and Shine had already discovered that apart from the major and the colour sergeant and a couple of other NCOs none of this lot had ever been part of a ship's company in the proper sense, the peacetime sense. They had all been trained as commandos pure and simple and their only experience of the hogwash had been in small stuff, landing craft and suchlike, so they were not even half proper matlows. Still, they had a job to do and no doubt they would do it all right.

Blockship! What an end for the poor old *Castile*. Bullshit Shine's thoughts went back to his last commission aboard the light cruiser. Malta, too many years ago to be thought about. The Grand Harbour crammed with the ships of the Mediterranean Fleet – the battle squadrons, C-in-C's flag flying in the old *Queen Elizabeth*, battle-cruisers, aircraft-carriers, cruisers . . . the destroyers and submarines lying in Sliema Creek. Nights ashore, taking a *dghaisa* from the *Castile* to Custom House steps below the shore signal station.

Shine turned, hearing a step behind him. It was Mr Marty. Mr Marty who had been in Malta with him at the time, part of the Med Fleet but not in the *Castile*. Marty laid a hand on Shine's shoulder, grinned and sang, not untunefully, in a low voice, a fragment of a well remembered ditty.

'You may pass,
Kiss my arse,
Make fast the *dghaisa*. . . .'

'Two minds with but a single thought, sir,' Shine said.

'That's right. Nights up the Gut!'

Shine gave a short laugh. 'The Gut, eh.' Bars and prozzies. Not to mention fairies. Strada Stretta, to give the Gut its proper name, was legendary to the British Navy. Every other building a bar, many of them named patriotically after British warships. And the women, the second lure for the libertymen. Many fat and forty, but plenty of young stuff, lithe, lissome, dark and sultry, who

82

knew all the tricks of their trade and were not expensive. It was true that a spell in Malta always meant plenty of work for the quacks aboard the ships, whose surgeries became little more than VD clinics, but this didn't seem noticeably to lessen the trade of the Gut. Once bitten twice shy, but there was always a first time and there were literally thousands of seamen moving in and out of Malta, new ships arriving, replacement drafts from the manning ports at home, and so on.

'Great days,' Mr Marty said.

'Yes. And now a rotten end for this poor old tub.'

'No, I don't agree, old son. Go out in glory . . . a sight better'n ending up in the breakers' yard.'

'Glory, eh! Torn to shreds by the Jerries' gunfire.' With Arthur Marty, unlike with the ordinary seamen, Shine was able to let his hair down a little. 'Not that we won't do our best to bloody survive!'

'That's right. Do our best, for the old ship's sake. I reckon we all will. Us old hands – and the others, of course.' Marty paused. 'What the skipper said . . . this job's vital. It's an honour for the old *Castile*.'

Shine said thoughtfully, 'You could be right at that.' As he moved away along the upper deck, checking on all gun positions and stepping irritably over recumbent commandos for whom there was no room below, Shine reflected on that broadcast from the bridge. Blockship in Dieppe, a port quite handily constructed for being blocked in: there was an elbow twist in the entry, and beyond this lay most of the port installations. Not only the port installations, Cameron had said. Intelligence sources had indicated a build-up of super-fast, super-large, ocean-going motor torpedo-boats, really big stuff, much bigger and more seaworthy than the E-boats that were in the habit of attacking the coastal convoys passing up and down the North Sea – and God knew they had caused enough damage, sinkings and casualties to hard-to-replace merchant seamen, to say nothing of the losses to the escorts, the corvettes and armed

83

trawlers. The E-boats were sods enough: in Dieppe were those much bigger sods, said to be of more than 100 tons, 120 feet in length, well armed with 22m guns and 40mm cannon, carrying six torpedoes of the homing-in variety, and capable of up to some 45 knots. Their destiny would be to move out across the North Atlantic to back up the U-boats and, cruising in formidable groups, speed in among the ships of the ocean convoys, many of them bringing US troops across from the other side.

'They have to be hemmed in,' Cameron had said on the Tannoy. 'Do that, and maybe thousands of lives will be saved. As you all know, the U-boat campaign against the convoys in the North Atlantic hasn't been having so much success lately – we've hit the U-boat packs to an extent unacceptable to the German Naval Command. These new craft are their answer.' Cameron had paused there. 'Mr Churchill is taking a personal interest in our mission. He hasn't forgotten what the U-boats were achieving until recently. Massive sinkings . . . he doesn't want to see the Battle of the Atlantic go the other way again now. You all know what happens if the convoys don't get through: starvation within a matter of a couple of weeks. And no more US troops and weapons and ammo coming through. We're being relied on to fight the ship through whatever they throw at us . . . fight through and put our nose into the dock wall. While we were in Scapa, the bow section for'ard of the seamen's mess was packed with high explosive, set with primers and detonators. That will act not only to damage the entrance itself but will also act as a scuttling charge. What's left will block the fairway.'

He had gone on to say that the *Castile* was scheduled to make a landfall off the coast of France at midnight in a little over twenty-four hours' time. Before that there would be a call at Barry in the Bristol Channel: this would be in the nature of a red herring for the benefit of any Nazi agents who might be watching the ship's progress. *Castile* would leave Barry under escort of a single destroyer, ostensibly

84

for Portsmouth but would alter for Dieppe after passing to the south of the Needles. The destroyer would accompany the mission and would stand off ready to come in and take off the ship's company of the *Castile* after completion.

'Survivors,' Chief PO Froggett said to Leading Seaman Pafford. 'If any!'

'Done any blockship time, buff?' Pafford asked slily.

'Do me a favour,' Froggett said irritably. To his knowledge, the last blockship had been the old *Vindictive* around a quarter of a century earlier: blockships and their activities were not an integral part of naval warfare these days. But he did remember the débâcle at Dieppe when, supported by a small force of US Rangers, a combined British and Canadian landing had been attempted under the aegis of Mr. Churchill and Lord Louis Mountbatten in – when was it now? – August 1942. The slaughter had been horrific, and nothing whatsoever achieved – except a certain knowledge that Dieppe was no easy target. Why couldn't the motor torpedo-boats and their perishing base be attacked from the air, had been Froggett's immediate thought during Cameron's broadcast, and Cameron himself had answered that in the course of his spiel: the vessels were hidden away in bomb-proof pens, and RAF attempts to block the fairway had met with no success at all. There had been very heavy losses resulting in nothing more than a few chunks of cliff and rock dislodged.

So once again it was up to the navy. Up to the old *Castile*. Glory, in the somewhat sardonic words of Mr Marty, lay ahead.

ii

Glory didn't mean a lot to Ordinary Seaman MacTavish: he simply didn't think in terms of glory as applied to any situation in which he might find himself. There was not much glory to be found in the Gorbals or indeed in any of the sleazier entrails of Glasgow, although there had been plenty of pride in the distant past, the sailing of Scots-manned ships from the Broomielaw to all parts of the world. There had been much pride in the great ships built in the Clyde shipyards. A decline had come in the thirties: no work for thousands, one of whom had been MacTavish senior who hadn't even got a job when the work returned with the recommencement of work on Job Number 534, later to be named as the *Queen Mary*. MacTavish's father had become over-addicted, in the better years, to his whisky and chaser, and he'd become known as the man who tended to drop hammers in awkward places where they hit other men, and who was unsteady with a rivet gun. Of course, with the war a kind of prosperity had returned to the Clyde but by this time MacTavish senior had been pushing up the daisies, dead of drink, which left young MacTavish with a mother to support, a task he now shared with two sisters who did the donkey work of the day-to-day routine – Mrs MacTavish was bedridden with leg ulcers.

Not much glory there either.

Nor any glory in being unemployed pre-war: young MacTavish hadn't followed his father into the shipyards. He had no stomach for that. So when the call-up came, he couldn't plead a reserved occupation and was hauled off willy-nilly into His Majesty's Navy. They'd talked, rather tongue-in-cheek, about glory in the training establishment, which had been HMS *Ganges* at Shotley, the same place as Jimmy the One, Lieutenant Brown, had started his career. But in MacTavish's case the references to glory – largely in regard to the navy's past, the Armada, the Glorious First of June, Nelson and Trafalgar, Sturdee and the Battle of the Falkland Islands, Jellicoe and Beattie – had fallen upon sullenly deaf ears while Ordinary Seaman MacTavish thought back to his own glories, the knuckle-duster and the knife, the bicycle chain and the razor-blade, the nails in thrown potatoes, the ball bearings to scatter the police horses and break their legs and bring their riders down helplessly. That had been MacTavish's war.

86

And yet there was something else: MacTavish had a deep hatred for the Nazis. He had encountered Sir Oswald Mosley's thugs in the Glasgow streets, a riot in George Square when he'd been done over by the Mosleyites, left almost for dead, covered with blood from a dozen wounds, an arm and a leg broken. A mate with him had suffered irreversible brain damage. Physically MacTavish had mended, but the mental scar was very deep. The result of that began to come home to roost shortly after Cameron's broadcast. MacTavish had not so far seen the enemy, had not been in any kind of action. He'd just plodded the seas on the convoy escorts and had been lucky, and also very chokker. Life had been both hard and dull, and not enough money.

Now, suddenly, it was going to be different.

MacTavish looked down from his gun as a voice addressed him: Bullshit Shine, fresh from his talk with Mr Marty and with glory on his mind.

'You, MacTavish.'

'Aye . . . chief.' MacTavish wanted to say 'sod off' but didn't.

'That charge. Returning aboard drunk. Insurbordinate language to an officer. Right? Nasty. Nasty for you, that is. But officers is human.'

'Is that right?'

'It's right, MacTavish. Do your best when we're in the thick of it, and maybe it'll rub off. No promises, mind.'

MacTavish said, 'Aye. D'ye mean you think I'll not do ma –'

'I don't think,' Bullshit Shine said crisply. 'I'm not paid to think. I have to bloody *know*. And I know you'll come up smiling, sonny boy, because you're a Scot. Like that bloke Robert the Bruce.'

Shine walked away. MacTavish said, 'Jesus Christ' in a tone of amazement and turned back to his gun. Sassenachs were a weird bunch, right enough. MacTavish wracked his brains, trying to recall what Robert the Bruce had done.

Won a battle, or something. Against the English. Waterloo? No. Culloden? MacTavish hadn't had much schooling. In the end he settled for Preston Pans . . . there was also Bannockburn but it was a Sassenach, King Alfred, who'd burned the cakes. . . .

iii

'Worst bloody job in the Andrew,' Chief Stoker Rump said bitterly to Chief ERA Hollyman. 'For us, anyway.'

'Could be worse on the upper deck, Rumpo. All them bullets flying about.'

'You know what I mean.'

'Yes, you're right, I do.' Hollyman thought about incarceration in the racket and heat of the engine spaces, the shafts kept turning until the very last moment, the moment of impact, the moment of explosion and a glimpse of hell. With any luck they wouldn't still be down there: the bridge should pass the order to clear the engine-room and boiler-rooms and leave everything set to full ahead, but it would be a close judgment since the skipper would need to have manoeuvrability until not far off the end, might even need to turn short round for some reason, in the port's constriction, which would mean engine movements – say, full ahead port, full astern starboard to assist the rudder and decrease the turning circle. If the skipper got it wrong they would all fry. The explosion in the bows, the tremendous impact, would work right through the ship to the engine spaces and they might crumple, the network of steel ladders, those that led to the airlock and a sort of safety, all twisted up like a spider's-web gone wrong. Also, of course, there would be the gunfire from the shore, and there might even be the *Luftwaffe* swooping in with its bomb loads. Or perhaps not: they might be getting air cover – the skipper hadn't said they would, though. . . .

For this, unknown to Hollyman and Rump, there was a good reason: on embarking, Major Wilson of the

88

commando unit had told Cameron that there would be no air cover.

'Somewhat sudden, isn't it?' Cameron had said in surprise. 'The orders I was given –'

'Change of mind, Captain. Air Ministry. They're playing down Dieppe. There's to be a diversionary raid, a heavy one, on Calais. Another on Cherbourg. Timed for shortly before our entry to Dieppe.'

'Churchill?'

'Mr Churchill's said to be in full agreement. He says the navy can cope.' Wilson lifted an eyebrow at Cameron. 'It can – can't it?'

'It seems it'll damn well have to, doesn't it?' Cameron snapped. In his view this was the RAF all over again: pull out and leave the sailors and soldiers to it. Yet, this time, there was logic: a diversion would be no bad thing. If the defence of Dieppe slacked off, if Goering diverted his fighter aircraft to Calais and Cherbourg, it would help. But the naked feeling would be with them all at Dieppe. The RAF could on occasions provide a welcome umbrella. A safe feeling, like a sturdy roof. Later, as the *Castile* came down past Liverpool Bay, Cameron was aware of Lieutenant Batten studying the shore through his binoculars. There was light coming into the sky now and the buildings were beginning to stand out: the port installations, the huge warehouses and stores of the Mersey Docks and Harbour Board, and the Liver Building with its vast stone Liver Birds. Distant, but close to the heart of any Liverpudlian.

Batten turned and met Cameron's eye.

'It brings it all back,' he said.

'I'm sure it does, Pilot. If I was to sail past Aberdeen – ' Cameron bit back on his tongue. That was nobody's business but his and it was better the ship's company didn't know the Captain had anything on his mind but the job in hand.

'Sir?' Batten was looking puzzled.

'Never mind, Pilot. Not important.'

A father was a father but he wasn't a wife. Fathers grew old in the normal course of events, and in the normal course of events they died. You missed them, but there it was. A young wife should have her whole life before her; the loss was a tragedy. Batten's face was bleak, his mouth set hard. He was another of the *Castile*'s company with a personal hatred for the Nazis and all they stood for. The light cruiser passed on, down to the Skerries, and Liverpool faded. Cameron paced the bridge, dead tired and keeping moving so as to keep awake as he had been all through the night, with Batten. Major Wilson had gone below to get his head down in Cameron's cabin aft: at sea, Cameron used his sea cabin just below the bridge – but in pilotage waters the Captain's place was on the bridge itself. During the dark hours at any rate . . . when the dawn had filled the sky the First Lieutenant came up the ladder, seaboots clattering on the metal treads.

'Time for some kip, sir. I'll take over.'

'I'm all right, Number One.'

'It's all plain sailing from here down to the Bristol Channel. You're going to need to be fresh later on, sir.'

Cameron nodded: it made sense. 'All right, Number One. Call me in accordance with Standing Orders and in any case as soon as we bring St Govan's abeam.' He turned to the navigator. 'You too, Pilot. Send down for Blake to take over OOW – he'll be all right.'

He went down to his sea cabin, stripped off duffel coat, monkey-jacket and seaboots and turned in all standing thereafter. He was dead asleep within a minute.

iv

Cameron was on the bridge again as the *Castile* turned to port to enter the Bristol Channel. Later they lay-to off the port of Barry, in the lee of the heights of Barry Island, pre-war Mecca of holiday-making miners from the valleys.

As they waited for the destroyer to emerge from the lock, Cameron looked across at the big ordnance depot at Sully, a place crammed with the munitions of war, mainly from the USA, and beyond it Sully Island and Flatholm . . . it was raining now, a dirty penetrating drizzle as so often in Wales. Everything was damp and depressing and now Cameron ached to be away and heading for his objective: the sooner they could get there, the sooner it would be over, though he knew he couldn't arrive before the set time for the operation.

'*Dionysus* coming out, sir.'

'Thank you, Yeoman.' Cameron waited until the destroyer was clear of the lock and turning to go ahead of the *Castile* for the outward passage. When she was some four cables off, he passed the orders to the wheelhouse and engine-room and the *Castile* turned for the open sea. The rain was heavy now, and a fresh wind had come up. This was in accordance with the weather forecast, and bad weather was predicted for the area between Newhaven and Dieppe. A little luck was with them already; Cameron was tempted to take this as a harbinger. So was Mr Marty, going round what was left of his main armament, checking on the guns with Lieutenant Blake, now relieved of the bridge watch.

'Bugger up the Nazis, I reckon, this weather, bugger 'em up nicely, Mr Blake.'

'I hope you're right, Guns.' Blake was a little white around the gills, Marty noticed.

'Nothing to worry about.'

'I'm not worried.' Blake was edgy.

'No, course not. I didn't mean you was worried, not like that, you know what I mean.'

'That's all right, Guns.' Blake moved on, doing his best to look efficient and knowledgeable, right on top of his job as gunnery officer, glad that the chief gunner's mate was doing something somewhere else around the ship: Shine had a way of looking at you that was very off-putting. And

Peter Blake had other worries, home worries that had come in that mail delivery back in Scapa. In Bodmin, Mary Anne was on the sick list. There had been a long letter from her mother and reading between the lines Blake had been in no doubt that his mother-in-law was blaming him for her daughter's illness, which had not yet been diagnosed. The doctors were so busy, there was a shortage of them and since the younger ones had gone off to the war the old ones had been left to carry on, some of them having been dug out of retirement. There was a hint that Blake should by now have provided Mary Anne with a home of her own – much though the Larkspurs liked having her to themselves, of course, he wasn't to think they didn't – which would have helped. Why? Reading on distractedly, Blake discovered that Mary Anne's illness was to do with depression. Doctors, Mrs Larkspur wrote, didn't take depression seriously and she had been told to see to it that Mary Anne bucked herself up, took a grip. In the meantime she was losing weight, had a peaky look, wouldn't eat, sat about listlessly. Mrs Larkspur was very worried indeed and what was he going to do about it?

Peter Blake, gunnery officer of what was set to become a blazing wreck, thought sardonically about what he could do: leap overboard and swim for the shore, send a telegram to the Admiralty saying he'd had enough and was needed at home, tell Churchill he would have to carry on the war without his assistance? In all conscience, that was about the sum of what was open to him.

Bullshit Shine marched up, halted smartly. 'All right, sir?'

Mr Marty said, 'Everything on the top line, GI.'

'That's good.' Shine's face tilted up and his gaze raked Peter Blake. The officer looked like what the buzz said he was, an estate agent's runner marooned aboard a warship, poor sod. He was going to need nursing along when the fun started . . . fun! Even Bullshit Shine didn't much like the jocular word. Blockships were no fun at all. He started in

92

on the nursing. 'We'll blast 'em for six, sir, you mark my words. Them guns is good. Right, Mr Marty, sir?'

Marty nodded. 'Right, GI.' He didn't go on to say they were good for just so long as they were there behind their gunshields. Or that that length of time was problematic. Or that once in there could be no turning back. Blake could work that out for himself; and Blake did. He felt his stomach loosen as the *Castile* moved on westwards through the Bristol Channel, to the north of Bodmin beyond Exmoor's forest-clad hills. By this time tomorrow Mary Anne might have a lot more to worry about, and he didn't feel life would be good for her, back entirely in her mother's arms.

8

DURING HIS briefing at the Admiralty
Cameron had been told that there would be help from the
French Resistance, the *maquis*, inside Dieppe. Already the
local Resistance leaders had backed up the aerial
reconnaissance reports by giving information via the
concealed transmitters, passing exact locations of the Nazi
MTB pens together with the quickest route to be used by
the commandos for the job they had to do, which was not,
in fact, to mount an attack on the bomb-proof pens
themselves; they had a separate assignment that carried a
very high security classification. Cameron, who had been
given the full facts, made no mention of the task awaiting
the commandos when, on speaking to his ship's company,
he told them of the Resistance, men ready to mount their
own diversion and attack the Nazi port guards when the
time came.

'Frogs,' an AB named Bottomley said, blowing his nose
over the side, closing one nostril with his thumb to give
extra impetus to the one to be cleared. ''Arf the buggers
are on 'Itler's side anyway. Can't trust Frogs . . . met 'em
before, I have. In this ship an' all. Up the straits,' he added,
in reference to the Mediterranean station. 'We was showing
the flag, like. Went into bloody Monte Carlo, we did. There
was a Frog cruiser in. Cor! talk about booze. Them Frogs

94

bloody bathed in vino, pissed as newts all along the waterfront.'

'And you were stone cold sober, Stripey?' It was Ordinary Seaman Quentin who asked the question, playing along since no-one else bothered to take up anything Stripey Bottomley – Stripey on account of the three good-conduct badges on his left arm – said, Stripey being exceptionally garrulous and repetitive.

'Course I bloody wasn't, young twerp,' Stripey said. ''Ood be sober in Monte, eh? But I wasn't as pissed as them buggers, nothing like.'

'Well? What happened?' Quentin pulled the hood of his duffel coat closer round his face: the wind was keen and there was a slop of water coming aboard, with spray blowing aft from the bows as the *Castile* dipped her head under.

'Got into a fight,' Stripey said succinctly. 'Then nearly got arrested. Nearly but not quite. I did a bunk and nipped down into a boat waiting to go off to one of them steam yachts that the nobs cruised around in. French nob this one was as it 'appened, Duke de something or other –'

'How did you find that out?'

'Cos I got took off to the yacht when a bunch o' floosies came aboard the boat be'ind me. Giggling at me . . . you know what I mean, thought I was a bloody joke, something to while away the boredom of 'aving too much money. It was like that, back in the twenties, son. Flappers, they called 'em in England. Spend, spend, spend, always on the lookout for something different. Well, in Monte that was me.' A backward look came into Stripey Bottomley's eye. 'Mind, I was younger then, a lot younger. Slim an' all.'

'What's that got to do with it?'

'Plenty,' Stripey answered. 'I was took out to the anchorage and aboard the yacht, kind of kidnapped like, though I wasn't complaining, not with the Frog police on the jetty. Anyway, there I was, in the lap o' luxury. Gold taps in the bathrooms . . . bidets . . . me'ogany furnishing

95

inlaid with sort of posh-coloured wood . . . sofas an' that
. . . beds, not bunks. Thick carpets, plenty of booze going
free, an' all them girls, *Frog* ones. One of 'em said she'd
always wanted to do it with an English sailor. In public. I
told you they was bored, too much time on their 'ands.'

'And did you?'

'No,' Stripey said after a moment. 'I bloody didn't. I
would 'ave . . . they all got round me and got me clothes
off, clapping and giggling like a lot o' chorus girls. Didn't
take me long to show 'em I was ready. See?'

'Ye-es. . . .'

'Know what they did?'

'What?' Quentin asked.

'They 'ung a rosary on it and then rang for the deck'ands
and 'ad me thrown overboard with me uniform slung round
me neck in a bundle. Got back aboard the old *Castile*
soaked through after bloody near drowning – wasn't far off
the *Castile*, that yacht, which was a bit o' luck. Told the
Officer o' the Watch I'd fell in, which was partly true.
Anyway – that's why I says, you can't trust Frogs. An' now
the skipper, 'e says we 'ave to deliver ourselves right into
the 'ands of a bunch o' Froggies waiting in Dieppe –'

'With a rosary?' Quentin asked, straight faced.

'Don't be bloody impertinent to your elders, sonny.'

ii

France and the French were different now: after years of
the Nazi occupation dalliance was a thing of the past. To
work against Hitler was the first preoccupation. The men
and women were in it together, facing the daily possibility
of capture, torture and death, perhaps in the concentration
camps and the gas chambers of the Third Reich. Constantly
there were disappearances, swoops from the Gestapo made
without warning, sometimes as a result of information laid
by fellow Frenchmen, supporters of the Vichy government.
But always there were more of the *maquis* to step as it were

96

into the firing line, to prepare the booby traps that killed arrogant Nazi officers and troops, to ambush the ammunition trains, to hide the illegal receivers and transmitters that formed the link with London, to pass information and arrange drops and pick-ups from British aircraft as agents were brought in or taken out.

The occupation forces were under constant surveillance and as many Germans as Resistance fighters had suddenly disappeared whilst on guard duty, or walking the streets, or disporting themselves with apparently compliant French-women. The rosary had gone, along with so much else; it had been replaced by the knife, the garrotte, the butcher's cleaver, the silenced revolver. In the port of Dieppe, as the *Castile* headed in for the coast of France through disturbed seas and the onset now of the dark, Nazi troops marched their guardposts in the docks and along the railway line leading from the old cross-channel ferry berths to Rouen and Paris. And each of those sentries, so unsuspecting of what was about to break over his head, was a marked man.

iii

At home in England the thoughts of the families were sporadically with the *Castile*: sporadically because it was not in human nature to worry the whole of the long time between leaves. There was so much else to do in wartime Britain. The constant battle with the ration books, the coupons and the points, the difficulty of arranging a wardrobe with the so few clothing coupons, to say nothing of the food situation. Everything in short supply, eggs a rarity, tiny chunk of butter to last a week, scarcely any cheese, chops and sausages worth their weight in gold when they could be got. Blackouts and officious Air Raid Wardens, the bombs on so many parts of the country, the nights spent in the Anderson shelters or, in London, on the deep tube-station platforms where the actual passengers, largely service personnel coming and going on leave through the main line stations, could hardly move along for the press of bodies – men, women and children trying to find sleep with pillows and mattresses and blankets all over the show, tired, squalling children, fractious old-timers, weary and anxious mothers trying to hold a family together while the men were away at the war, or rather their side of the war for this time everyone was at war, home front as well as overseas.

In the officers' club in Portsmouth Evelyn Brown, captain's daughter and lieutenant's wife, carried on her war in a degree of comfort: servicemen's clubs were treated a little more leniently when it came to supplies, and there was always a fair quota of alcohol and cigarettes, the sinews of life that kept men sane in war. The flat in Fareham drew a proportion of its supplies from the club.

As the *Castile* steamed on for her objective, Evelyn got into an Austin Seven waiting outside the club: day's work done early, and a major from the ordnance depot at Hilsea who had been able to wangle some petrol, since on occasions he used his own car for duty.

'Tired?' he asked sympathetically.

'Damn tired, Andy.' She closed her eyes, rubbed at them as the car moved away to head past the Hippodrome and the Guildhall for North End and Cosham, through Wymering, past the Harbour Lights public house, now with no lights showing from Portsmouth Harbour. The war had made everything eerie and at the start unfamiliar, though by now they were all used to it, used to groping about darkened streets, used to cars with their headlamps blanked off except for narrow slits to make them visible to pedestrians. Not that there were many cars except for staff cars from the various service establishments, and of course military transport, lorries filled with soldiers or sailors on draft or being taken to and from fire-watching duties in the dockyard warehouses or the goods depot at Fratton railway station. The Nazis were fond of dropping incendiary bombs as well as high explosive, and there was a lot at risk in a town like Portsmouth, premier naval port of the Empire.

The car stopped outside the flat, which was in an early Victorian house at the eastern end of the High Street. The major got out, came round and opened the door.

'Thanks, Andy.'

'That's all right.' He hesitated, fiddling with his cane. 'May I – er – come in, Eve?'

She nodded. 'Why not? It's lonely. There's a little gin, I think. No whisky.'

They went inside: the flat was the ground floor. The major, who hadn't been inside before, looked around appreciatively. The rooms were nicely proportioned . . . so was Evelyn Brown. He asked, 'Husband been away long?'

'Most of the time we've been married, except for leaves. He had a short leave a fortnight ago.'

'Uh-huh. As you said – lonely, isn't it?'

'Yes. You too, I'd have thought. Why not get your wife down here?'

He said, taking a glass of gin, 'Danger. She's safe where she is, touch wood.' The major's home was a village in Wiltshire. It was a training area so there were military targets, but not too near the village, and in any case Goering hadn't been active around Salisbury Plain. Probably too much open ground . . . the major, glad enough to have his wife and domestic chores a good distance away, asked, 'What ship's the old man in, Eve?'

She told him, without much interest. A ship was a ship and so far as she knew he was somewhere up north, a long way from the bombs unless he was on the Clyde – John never went into details, being a conscientious and security-minded officer. But he would be all right: he was that sort, always came through. Sometimes, guiltily, she saw a different future for herself if anything should happen. John was dull, too service minded, too unimaginative, in bed and out of it. She gave a little giggle as she recalled a story about how gunners' mates did it – by numbers, like gun drill.

99

'What's the joke?'

She told him. He laughed and said, 'Regimental sergeant-majors have a similar reputation.'

'And majors?' There was a glint in her eye. Why be lonely? You didn't have to be, and the major had sex appeal in a dark sort of way – thick black hair, neat moustache, hairy wrists. She had already seen that he was very willing to cope with a woman's loneliness.

iv

Next morning at 0730 hours the major left and drove back to Hilsea in his Austin Seven, a date arranged for that night. And that night, as once again the car stopped outside the Fareham flat, Lieutenant John Brown climbed to the bridge of *Castile* and spoke to Cameron.

'Four hours, sir?'

'That's it, Number One. I'll close up to full action stations in two hours' time. How are the commandos?'

'In the way,' Brown said with feeling. 'I'll be glad when they go below.' The orders were that the commandos, once the whole ship's company was at first degree of readiness, would be packed down in the after flat like sardines in a tin to be out of the way of the *Castile*'s gunners and also to keep in cover until the ship was ready to disembark them. No point in having them exposed to the Nazi gunfire during the dangerous business of port entry. The disembarkation would be a case of a leap for the jetty; and it would be made as soon as the *Castile*'s bows were embedded and the explosive charges had gone up, a concerted rush as if from out of the fires of hell as Mr Marty had expressed it in conversation with Peter Blake.

'Ladies from hell,' Mr Marty said.

'That was the kilted Scots, Guns.'

'Yes, I know. But didn't you see the pipes, eh, when they come aboard off Lamlash?'

Blake shook his head. He had been preoccupied, not thinking about bagpipes.

'Well, I did. I had a word with the colour sergeant. He has a piper . . . attached from the army, from the Argylls. They're going to do it in style.'

In style. In style amid the hail of bullets from rifles and machine guns, grenades, steel-helmeted Huns, maybe even light artillery in support, even tanks. Dieppe wasn't going to be undefended. In Blake's view that piper wasn't going to last half a minute. Probably none of them would last much longer. The least that could happen was that the survivors would end up as prisoners-of-war, and that wouldn't be much help to Mary Anne either. At that moment, although this could not be known to Peter Blake except as a matter of deduction, Mary Anne was in bed in the Larkspurs' house in Bodmin. In bed but wide awake and her face haunted. She had switched on the bedside light behind the thick blackout; she couldn't bear the dark, all of a sudden, she didn't know why. There was menace in it somehow, it had had to be dispelled . . . like Evelyn Brown for different reasons, Mary Anne too was a prey to loneliness even though her parents were close around her. Rather obviously so : she heard footsteps along the landing outside her room, and then a little later the flushing of the lavatory cistern, a sound like Niagara Falls in the otherwise silent night. Dad : if the doctors had been less hard-worked, he would have had a prostate operation by now. He was always spending pennies, or, as he put it himself when forced to refer to it at all, Making Water. It was a continuing nuisance, because the least sound woke Mary Anne when she wasn't already awake.

She found she was shaking all over. Not from cold – it wasn't cold. An awful feeling overcame her, that terrible depression again, something she was quite unable to shake off. Of course, it was the war and Peter being away in that ship and she not knowing exactly where he was or when he would be home again, if ever. The depression was linked with a kind of claustrophobia. Mary Anne switched off the light, then went to the window and pulled back the blackout

101

curtains. There was a moon, and it lit on Victoria Barracks not far away, high up on a hill, the depot of the Duke of Cornwall's Light Infantry, and in front of it the 1914–18 War Memorial to the men of the regiment who'd died in those dreadful years. When this one was over, there would be a lot more names. . . .

Mary Anne let out a cry, a deep and rending sob that seemed to come involuntarily from her throat. A few moments later the door came open: her mother.

'What is it, darling?'

'I – I don't know.' She clung to the windowsill as though it was a rock of safety. Mrs Larkspur gave a clicking sound and came across the room, fast in the moonlight coming through the bare window, took Mary Anne by the shoulders, gently. She smelled of bed and was in heavy metal curlers. 'There, there,' she said. 'Did Dad wake you, is that it?'

'No.'

'I keep telling him but he takes no notice.'

'I said he *didn't* wake me!' Mary Anne clenched her fists and thumped them on the windowsill. 'I'm all right, Mum. Just leave me alone, for God's sake!'

'Well, I must say!' Mrs Larkspur stood back, bewildered, hurt, anxious. 'Don't go and do anything stupid, darling, that's all.'

'Like what?'

No answer; Mary Anne supplied her own. 'Like jump out of the window, I suppose.'

Still bewildered, Mrs Larkspur found inappropriate words. 'Well, you can't be too careful I always say.' She moved to the door. 'Call me at once if you want me, darling, won't you?'

'Yes!' Hysteria mounted, though as yet still under control. Mrs Larkspur shrugged and departed, closing the door quietly, then opening it a crack, just in case. Mary Anne stared from the window, seeing not Bodmin now but visions, waking visions of what she had seen in a dream,

102

horrible scenes of gunfire and flame, men shot to ribbons, a sinking ship way out on the ocean, far from help, and Peter calling to her, his face desperate and pleading, arms held out.

It was an omen – she knew that. She gave a high scream, and mother came back. This time, with her father, who, muttering about the blackout, switched off the light that Mrs Larkspur had just put on. Not a moment too soon: from below in the street came the angry bellow: 'Thank *you* very much indeed. Don't you know there's a war on?'

v

The night was very dirty now, with high, running seas and a half gale blowing. Spray was everywhere, and it was cold. On the bridge, the lookouts wore oilskins over their duffel coats, woollen gloves on the hands that held the binoculars; from the guns, the white anti-flash gear over the faces of the gunnery rates showed ghostlike through the gloom. Yeoman of Signals Robbins was on the flag deck, ready for anything though he didn't reckon there would be any visual signalling that night, not even with *Dionysus*, the destroyer that was keeping station three cables astern. The ships were to remain unseen for as long as possible, naturally, creeping up on the occupied coast of France. According to what Robbins had overhead from the officers, *Castile* was now some fifteen miles off her target. Robbins ran a hand over the woodwork, the teak guardrail of the flag deck. The same wood, and never mind refits in the years between, as had been there when he'd served that earlier commission. He knew that for sure because as a leading signalman he'd carved a set of initials: not his own, but those of a young woman, the one who had become his wife, now dead by courtesy of a Portsmouth Corporation trolley-bus. He had been devoted to Dorothy and in a curious kind of way he felt close to her again now through the medium of those initials carved so long ago. It was as though he was meant to be back with them again, that maybe he would die with his hand on them. Along with all the rest of the ship's company he knew, now, beyond doubt that the old *Castile* wasn't meant to return across the channel. So at last, in a Nazi-occupied port, those lovingly carved initials would be gone forever. *He* might return, of course. You never knew. And if he did, well, there might be Maggie to return to.

It wouldn't be the same, that went without saying, but it would be something. At least they both shared a love of Dorothy: the sisters had been very close.

For'ard by the gun-shields of the six-inch main armament, Chief Petty Officer Shine climbed up and laid a hand on the breech block of one of the guns and spoke to Leading Seaman Pafford, captain of the gun.

'Give the buggers hell,' he said. 'They're good guns.'

'Sure, GI. I'll keep firing till I get knocked off.' Pafford's voice was sardonic: he reckoned this was a suicide mission pure and simple. 'Hero to the bleeding end, that's me.'

'No need to take that tone, Leading Seaman Pafford. We all does our duty to the best of our ability. We won't let the old *Castile* down, eh?'

'Think she *knows*, do you, GI?'

Shine stared through the dark. 'Knows what?'

'That she's done for. That we're all bloody well barmy to be here at all.'

'That's enough o' that,' Shine said crisply, and made his way aft, once again blaspheming as he tried to keep his feet clear of recumbent commandos or their weapons. He was thinking, perhaps the old ship does know. They always likened ships to women; that was partly a load of sentimental crap, of course . . . but there was something in it. When you got to know a ship really well, you could feel a soul in her, something living, something spiritual, a kind of oneness not to be rationally explained. Currently the *Castile* was proceeding at half speed only: the skipper, Shine guessed, was a little ahead of his ETA and was holding back. But it was almost as though the ship herself was

104

holding back, not from cowardice but from a natural desire not to end her life too soon. There was humanity in that. Bullshit Shine shrugged and went into the gunner's store to check on Leading Seaman Slugg's activities. He found Slugg in there, asleep on the deck with an arm curled around his head and his torso lying on a makeshift bed of old tarpaulins.

He woke him up with a prod of his seaboot.

'Up, Leading Seaman Slugg.'

'What is?'

'What is what?'

'Up, GI –'

'*You* will be if you don't watch it. Get your arse off the deck, pronto! Ship'll be in action any minute.'

Bollocks it will, Slugg thought mutinously, there's time yet for a kip. He got to his feet, stomach wobbling like a large jelly. Saliva had drooled down his cheeks to his blue overalls, a trail like that of a snail. Bullshit Shine peered about, looking for grounds for complaint and finding nothing. Or nothing much. Once again a seaboot prodded forward, towards something lying on the deck.

'What's that, Leading Seaman Slugg?'

Slugg said, 'Cat shit.'

'I know that, I'm not blind. Why is it there?'

'Cat done it. I didn't ask it why.'

'Bloody cat 'as no business in the gunner's store, Leading Seaman Slugg. Much less to shit in it. Clear it up, and see it don't occur again. Tell you something. If I comes across the perishing cat, I'll kick its arse over the side.'

Slugg knew he wouldn't do that: the GI was soft about the cat, say what he liked. Sometimes it slept in his hammock and Slugg, passing by the petty officers' mess when the door had been open, had heard daft conversations taking place. Puss puss, poor old pussy cat, come to daddy. The GI would have fed it goldfish if he'd had any. Slugg didn't know how the GI could bear to take it into action, into the concentrated fire of the Nazi hordes that awaited them, at any rate in Slugg's imagination. But of course any wartime voyage to sea could end in gunfire and sinking and if you had a cat at all then it had to take pot luck. And you had to have a cat: a ship without a cat was like a woman without a fanny. No pussy cat equalled bad luck.

Shine, leaving the gunner's store, was not thinking about cats; he was thinking about Rowlands Castle not all that far behind them as the crow flew. Rowlands Castle and Rosie. The village would be quiet now, all the pubs shut. Small village but four pubs – Fountain, Railway, Castle and Staunton Arms, and since the outbreak of war largely out of beer within an hour or so of opening in the evening. Shine could do with a pint now, Bass for preference. He licked his lips at the mere thought. And Rosie: she'd be tucked up in bed and missing his presence. Being a gunner's mate kept you fit and active, in good trim for the activities of the night, which Shine also missed at sea. The thought of this led him to the US Navy: he'd been aboard a US battleship once, in the Navy Operating Base at Norfolk, Virginia: walking round he'd been intrigued to see a brass tally over a door leading from the upper deck: Ladies' Retiring Room.

He'd thought that odd. Presumably even the Yanks didn't take women to sea. He'd asked his guide, an American PO, about that. The Yank had said, solemnly, that it was to fool the Krauts if ever they boarded. That was where they kept the secret codes and cyphers, the Yank said. Disguised as arse paper, very clever. Shine had had the feeling the Yank was taking the mickey, but he hadn't said anything because you never knew with Yanks. When they talked what you decided was tripe, it turned out to be for real. Also, the transatlantic terms were different: if you went into a stationery shop and asked for a rubber, you'd be told to go to the drugstore where you'd be given a french letter.

Yanks. Shine sucked at his teeth, dislodging supper from behind his plate. This war, they'd turned up trumps,

106

couldn't get by without them. Shine hated to admit that, being hidebound RN, but in all justice he did. His mind went back to Rosie again: she enjoyed walking in the country, and he'd come to enjoy it too, walking all the way from the Green, under the railway bridge, into Stansted Park, home of the Earl of Bessborough, right through the forest and back by way of Forestside village and Dean Lane End – back to the Castle for a couple of pints if he was lucky.

Good days: they might come again. Or they might not.

Bullshit Shine checked his wristwatch, holding it close to his eyes: half an hour off midnight. As he did so the Tannoy came on, the skipper himself speaking from the bridge.

'Hands to first degree of readiness. The ship will be off Dieppe in one hour's time. Action is expected to commence on entry. There will be no return fire until the order comes from the bridge. That is all.'

The Tannoy clicked off, a sound of finality.

9

THEY ALL KNEW the orders: in basis they were simple enough, very clear and direct. The guns were to blast away as soon as the gun-ready lamps glowed and the order came down. Targets: the shore batteries and searchlights for a start, after that anything that moved – aircraft, harbour boats, troop concentrations. For the rest of the upper deck personnel there would be little to do except muster aft away from the fo'c'sle that would take the impact and the explosion and then, when the final order came to abandon ship, to get over the side and swim towards the *Dionysus* who would have her scrambling-nets lowered ready to pick up the survivors and then turn and blast her away out to sea again. In the engine-room and boiler-rooms the black gang would have done its job a few minutes before the impact and with luck would have been ordered up from below.

Earlier, soon after the *Castile* had taken her last departure from the UK, John Brown had asked at what stage Cameron would give the order to abandon.

'Not as soon as you probably think, Number One.'

'Not right after we've hit the jetty?'

Cameron shook his head. 'No. That decision will have to be made a little later. Not too long, I hope. The commandos have to be given time, but. . . .' He turned to

108

Major Wilson. 'Perhaps you'd fill my First Lieutenant in yourself, Major.'

'Right.' Wilson spoke in a low voice, little more than a whisper, into Brown's ear. 'It's not an attack on the pens, they'll be effectively blocked. It's a cutting-out job.'

'Someone to be brought off?'

'Yes. An agent – one of ours. He's just one step ahead of the Nazis, they can't be allowed to get him. His own safety apart, he's badly wanted by Intelligence in London. It shouldn't take long. The Resistance chaps will be waiting outside the docks where the cross-channel ferries used to berth. Our man'll be with them.'

That was all the commando major had to say. Now, nearing Dieppe, it left Brown with plenty to think about as he made his own personal preparations for the final act of the *Castile*'s life. Shouldn't take long . . . there was always the unknown factor that ballsed-up the best of calculations. Someone being adrift, someone being shot, the Gestapo being more on the ball than expected, even a Frenchie overdoing the vino in a burst of patriotic fervour and joy. And if it did take at all long, the whole ship's company, and that of the *Dionysus* as well, would be at immense risk, fully exposed.

Brown stuffed his pockets from his cabin chest-of-drawers: nothing could be carried when they abandoned, no hand baggage. But there were the intimate valuables. A leather folding frame with a photograph of Evelyn went into Brown's inside pocket, plus in the other pockets a load of what most people would have called junk. A cheap propelling pencil, an elderly fountain pen given him by his mother one birthday, a handkerchief with lipstick on it – his wife's – a bundle of letters. Things like that.

It was much the same throughout the ship with the hands off watch before they were closed up at action stations. Chief PO Froggett also stowed away photographs – that was the first thought of the majority – and letters from his wife and children. Then the sentimental oddments, this, that and the other, things of value only to himself but bloody Hitler wasn't going to have them. Yeoman of Signals Robbins, who used his Signal Distributing Office as a personal caboosh, also sorted things out, going in from the flag deck for what might be a last look. A photo of Dorothy, very precious indeed – he could never get another now. He hadn't one of his sister-in-law and it wouldn't have been there with Dorothy if he had, it wouldn't have seemed right somehow. Not really. No letters in his case: no-one seemed to have bothered to write to him, except for the letter that had said his brother-in-law had died back in Pompey, and he'd torn that one up more or less automatically, seeing no point in keeping it. Little trinkets, mementos from the past: a matchbox holder inscribed with Chinese characters, given him by a girl in Hong Kong – he'd discovered afterwards that the Chinese characters formed a good luck message, and he'd never parted with it even now, long after the memory of the girl herself had faded.

Ordinary Seaman MacTavish, still under his cloud of Captain's Report, didn't bother because he hadn't anything. No photographs, no letters, nothing beyond his official uniform issue. He wasn't the sort to hang onto anything and no-one had ever given him anything to treasure anyway.

His personal collection made, Brown went back up to the bridge after another check around all the upper deck positions. His report made to the Captain, the next order was the one that had come when Bullshit Shine was checking his watch: action stations. One hour to go. As Cameron passed the word on the Tannoy, Brown gave an involuntary sigh.

Cameron glanced at him. 'Nostalgia, Number One?'

'Very much so. She was a good ship to me, the best. I'm going to hate it. Leaving her to the bloody Nazis, all shot to buggery.'

110

'I know how you feel.'

Brown gave a hard laugh. 'Not really, sir. You haven't served in her before. There's a difference.'

'Yes, I know. But . . . you know my father did, in the last lot.'

'Yes. Oh, there's a link all right, I do see that.'

Cameron said nothing further. This wasn't the time to go into death and bereavement – in all conscience, there would be more than enough of that very soon now. But suddenly he felt extraordinarily close to his father. He had felt it many times since leaving the anchorage in Scapa but now it was very strong. On this very bridge his father had stood as a lieutenant RNR, where Hugh Batten stood now, the navigating officer behind the binnacle at his action station. Aboard this very ship, his father had seen action so long ago. There was a strange feeling that his father was at his side, giving him strength to face up to his forthcoming responsibilities, the presiding over the death of the ship in such a way that in her final throes she would strike a blow against tyranny and oppression. And after that, to preserve his ship's company as best he knew how, remaining himself until the very end.

He would have liked to say all this to his First Lieutenant; but Brown might not really understand. And the bridge was not the place for what might be seen as sentimental maunderings.

ii

Below in the engine-room, Lieutenant(E) Rogers stood on the starting platform, hands clasped behind the back of spotless white overalls, a clean pair laid out by his steward in his cabin for the last hour of the *Castile*'s life. The chief engineer had to show proper respect for an old lady about to die. It so happened that Officers' Steward Crocker was also an old *Castile*, having served in her as a leading hand before being busted back to his present rate, in which he

111

had been recalled from reserve back in 1939. Crocker had been guilty of knocking off wardroom stores for his own consumption: it was a fair cop and he didn't complain, much. And he didn't blame the *Castile* for his lack of luck, because otherwise she had been a good ship and he'd had some very good months on the West Indies Station, based at Bermuda. The coal black mammies were good at what the shoregoing Crocker wanted and he suspected a number of little coffee-coloured bastards were growing to maturity in various West Indian islands, amid the palm trees and the blue seas and the sandy beaches, little bastards who would have no idea in the world of what daddy was facing now, which was a hero's death probably. In due course his name would likely be inscribed on the naval war memorial to the men of the Portsmouth Port Division on Southsea Common, those that had died in the last lot, but again the little bastards wouldn't know how honoured they were. Funny to think they might go to England one day, being half white, lucky little perishers, walk past that memorial, and never know. . . .

Talk about laugh. Of course, to them it was no laughing matter, being fatherless bastards, but if you didn't bloody laugh, as Crocker remarked to the ship's cat which came past at that moment, you'd bloody cry. Death was serious business so best not think about it too much.

'Same for you, mate,' he said to the cat, stroking it so that it arched its back, stretched up its neck, and purred. 'Poor little sod. Ought to 'ave put you off in the boat that brought them bootnecks, by rights.'

In his Crocker-produced clean overalls, Rogers was also thinking of past loves and in particular of the one who was likely to produce another little bastard, one that stood a very good chance of coming into the world totally fatherless. Rogers believed that you could as it were back date a child by subsequent marriage and that this would legitimize it. But you couldn't get married after death, a very final thing. A nasty thing, too, in an engine-room.

112

Rogers was a man of a certain amount of imagination and although he had never yet seen an engine-room that had taken a shell or a torpedo he could visualize it well enough. A red-hot hell swept through by blistering steam from fractured pipes, burned and scalded flesh, and a tangle of twisted steel ladders overhead, and no escape. In action, the engine-room was probably the worst place of all to be. But it was something that needn't last too long: when the water rushed in through the broken sides you would quite quickly drown, or what was left of you would.

Chief ERA Hollyman approached.

'All right, Chief?'

'All's well, sir, yes.' Hollyman paused. 'Rump's moaning, as usual. Chief Stoker, sir.'

'Yes, I'm aware of Chief Stoker Rump. What is it this time?'

'Piles, sir.'

Roger grinned. 'An appropriate malady in Rump's case. Has he seen the doctor?'

'Only just come on, sir. Like I said to him – it's too bleeding late now. If you get my meaning, sir.'

Rogers was about to make some further comment when the sound powered telephone from the bridge whined in his ear and he answered. 'Engine-room, engineer officer speaking.'

'I'm about to go up to full, Chief. All set?'

'All set, sir.'

'Seven miles to go. I'll let you know when we have the port entry in sight.'

'You haven't raised it yet?'

Cameron said, 'It's a murky night up here. That's no bad thing. Good luck, Chief.'

'And to you,' Rogers said. The phone went dead and he hung the instrument back on its hook. 'This is it,' he said to Hollyman, who nodded. A moment later the telegraph pointers moved and steadied on full ahead. Rogers lifted a hand and at once full power was fed through to the shafts.

113

In the boiler-room Chief Stoker Rump, cursing his sudden affliction, opened up the valves to send more oil fuel into the furnaces. The din below increased as the shafts came up to full, spinning in the great tunnels, and the *Castile* surged ahead, vibrating throughout her plates and carving a wide swathe through the disturbed waters of the channel.

iii

Ordinary Seaman Quentin felt the onset of fear, real fear. His stomach loosened. Not far off now and soon everything was going to be thrown at them. His fear was largely the fear of fear itself. As a candidate for a commission, fear was the last thing he must show; and Bullshit Shine would be the one to suss it out in no time if he did begin to show it. Bullshit Shine himself wouldn't know the meaning of fear, of course. He was made of steel, a robot in uniform, the perfect gunnery machine with a loud voice.

When at his gun a hand came down on his shoulder Quentin gave a start and turned, expecting to find the chief gunner's mate. He found Mr Marty, gunner RN, his warrant officer's stripe hidden by a massive amount of warm clothing that gave him more than ever the friendly shape of a bun.

'All right, lad?'

'Yes, sir, thank you.'

'Scared?'

'No, sir.' Quentin swallowed.

'Bollocks, course you're scared. So am I. Don't be afraid to admit it. That's half the battle, son. Admit it, face up to it, and tell yourself you'll come through without *acting* scared. That's the secret. Follow?'

'Yes, sir, I think I do.'

'That's the stuff. Know something? I wouldn't mind betting Nelson was scared stiff every time before action. Once it starts, it's different, you get carried away. I *know*. I was in the last lot, loading number in a 13.5-inch turret

114

aboard the old *Lion* – Admiral Beattie. I could count me heart-beats till the guns opened. After that I was too busy.'

Marty moved away. Quentin felt better in a sense, but he had another worry: why had the gunner picked on him? Had old Marty already sensed fear, did it show, or would he be saying the same thing to the other green hands, like MacTavish for instance, or Norton, or the other ordinary seamen, many of them facing their first experience of action? Quentin's mind went back into the past, not so long ago in fact. As an undergraduate at Cambridge he could never have visualized himself aboard a doomed light cruiser, heading through dirty weather for a French port in the hands of the Nazis, never have seen himself going through a hail of gunshot to end up in collision with a stone jetty and then an explosion. It was a different world, a different planet to an undergraduate. Quentin thought of the peaceful Cam, and punts, and girls, and bridges, of coffee at The Whim, of King's Parade and the shop where you bought college ties and scarves, of Market Square and its stalls, of bicycles, of Parker's Piece and Jesus Green and Addenbrooke's Hospital and the Fitzwilliam. He recalled his last interview with his tutor, after his call-up papers had come.

'A pity, Quentin. You were doing well.'

'Thank you, sir.'

'Of course, you have to answer the call. No question, I realize that. You wouldn't want to skrimshank. I wouldn't want you to. We have to win, in order to conserve all this.' The old boy had waved a hand in the air of his study, encompassing all Cambridge, the Cambridge that had been his life. 'We can't allow Attila the Hun to hold sway, can we?'

'No.'

'Of course, you'll find Philistines.'

'The Nazis?'

'No – oh, them too, of course. But you're going into the navy?'

'Yes, sir.'

'That's what I mean. Philistines. Sailors are not men of letters, Quentin, a rough, common lot in the main. But it's only temporary. We shall welcome you back to Cambridge when it's all over. Something to put behind you afterwards. In the meantime, good luck.'

Dry as dust, that elderly tutor, wreathed in pipe smoke. Public school in the dawn of history or not far off, then Cambridge as an undergraduate, then Cambridge again as a don. He'd never left the place except for an occasional bachelor walking tour of France, walking being his hobby, when term was down. A dull life; by now Quentin had experienced something so totally different that he was able to see Cambridge in some sort of perspective. Certainly sailors were not men of letters, much of their conversation being limited to, or anyway dotted with, four-letter words. Certainly they were Philistines when it came, say, to art appreciation, or a taste for the classics. Pin-ups were their art, nudes . . . most of the locker-lids along the messdecks had a voluptuous nude gummed to the inner side. Jolly Jack was ever one of the tits-and-bums brigade, and why not? Quentin grinned behind his gun shield: his old tutor, who had almost certainly never seen an example of either, would have blushed at the mere mention. Yes, sailors were a rough, common lot all right, none more so. But they were something else as well: they were men, and in the main goodhearted. Even Bullshit Shine was basically good-hearted, plenty of bark and when necessary plenty of bite as well, but not vindictive. If you had to die, well, you couldn't die in better company, if that was any consolation which it wasn't.

iv

'French coast in sight, sir.'

Cameron nodded. 'Thank you, Pilot. I've got it too.' He stared ahead through his binoculars. 'Tell the engine-room and wheelhouse.'

116

'Aye, aye, sir.' Batten passed the message down, then said, 'No reaction from the shore, sir.'

'Thanks to the Resistance. They'll have inhibited the radar installations – as planned. But we're going to be seen before much longer.' Cameron moved across the bridge to the telephone connecting with the director overhead. 'Stand by all guns, report when ready.'

Lieutenant Blake in the director acknowledged, and passed the order to the guns fore and aft. By this time the upper deck was clear of the commandos, packed tight below in the after flat and waiting the time to go. Blake reported back to the bridge.

'All guns ready, sir.'

'Thank you, Blake. Won't be long now.'

Still under full power, the *Castile* moved on. Soon the breakwater could be seen, a little on the port bow. Cameron passed the word down to the commandos: stand by but don't show yet. The First Lieutenant went aft to speak to the commando major. In the dim blue police lights in the after flat, the boot-polish-blackened faces looked ghostly. Mittened fingers clasped the dull metal of the sub-machine guns, knives were ready, grenades were at hand. The men, Brown thought, looked anxious to go now: there was a natural strain, but this would vanish in action.

'Good luck, Major,' Brown said.

'Thank you.' Briefly, the major grinned, white teeth in the blackened face. 'I trust we shall meet again!'

'Same here,' Brown said awkwardly. He had a strong feeling that he was speaking to a man already condemned to death. But for that matter, most of them probably were. There was an element of the Light Brigade: into the valley of death, drove the *Castile*. Guns to the left of them, guns to the right of them, volleyed and thundered. The thought had only just come into his mind when the thunder came from ahead, the crash of the German shore batteries opening up, and on their heels the whine of a shell travelling overhead.

Brown ran out of the after flat, along the upper deck for the bridge ladder. As he reached the foot of the ladder, the *Castile*'s six-inch guns opened and a blast of heat surged back from the fo'c'sle. Brown saw that the ship was almost at the harbour entry now, and the battle ensign had been hoisted. A second later there was an explosion on the arm of the breakwater as one of the six-inch shells took what had been a gun emplacement. A fire started and as the *Castile* plunged on Brown saw bodies lying about. From the fo'c'sle he heard a shout: Bullshit Shine.

'Well done, lads, that got the buggers where it hurts!'

Brown climbed the bridge ladder fast. Cameron was standing in the fore part, braced against the reinforced screen. Ahead, all hell had been let loose. The harbour seemed covered with tracer from close-range weapons, a spider's-web of fast-moving streaks of light. A shell came across the exposed bridge from the starboard side of the port entry: they could feel its wind, but it went away to port harmlessly. The *Castile*'s firing was kept up; Blake in the director at the foremasthead was pressing the firing button almost continuously, each time the gun-ready lamps came on. Brown looked over the fore screen: Mr Marty was with the chief gunner's mate, wiping spray from his face beneath his steel helmet. Now the ship was between the arms of the breakwater, well into the lee of the land.

Cameron said, 'Engines to half, Pilot.'

'Half ahead both, sir,' Batten said, and passed the order down. Some of the vibration went.

'Number One –'

'Sir?'

Cameron didn't finish what he had started to say. There was an explosion before the bridge, on the fo'c'sle by the for'ard six-inch. The gun remained intact: it had been only a small shell, but there were casualties. One of them was the gunner, lying on the deck with his head at a curious angle. Cameron said, 'Surgeon Lieutenant to go for'ard, Number One.'

118

10

Surgeon lieutenant David Ommanney was another RNVR. He had qualified MRCS, LRCP from Barts only eighteen months earlier and the *Castile* was his second naval appointment apart from his induction into the service at the Royal Naval Hospital at Haslar near Gosport. He had not seen action before, but the training at Haslar had been directed towards action and that training had been thorough. Many times Dr Ommanney had rehearsed in his mind what he would do in a host of situations: shell wounds, half severed arms and legs, burns, disembowelled stomachs, head injuries, chest injuries, torn windpipes, singly or all at once, all at once being the more likely, and all in the middle of continuing gunfire with, perhaps, the ship ablaze, and, if he was operating on deck, the ammunition exploding around him in the ready-use stowages. He had also, both in his last seagoing appointment and aboard the *Castile* whilst lying in Scapa Flow, carried out exercises, dummy runs in which his leading sick berth attendant had roped in spare hands to act as casualties to be swathed in bandages or splinted prior to being hauled up vertical ladders and through hatches in Neil Robertson stretchers.

Now it was different.

'Bag, sir,' the LSBA said, holding out Ommanney's action bag of tricks.

'What ?'

'Be needing it, likely, sir.' The LSBA paused, then added promptingly, 'Fo'c'sle, sir.'

'Yes.' Ommanney felt weak at the knees. He was afraid and didn't disguise the fact from himself, but there was something else: his first medical emergency as the MO in charge, at any rate on such a potential scale. He might not be able to cope: there was just the one of him, plus the LSBA. Ashore, say in a casualty department, he would have had all the assistance he needed, housemen, sisters, nurses, orderlies. All the latest equipment for saving life. Now he had just his bag. He took a grip and said, 'Right, come on.'

They left the wardroom, which was acting as a casualty clearing station and extended sick bay combined – the *Castile*'s actual sick bay was tiny, two cots, a makeshift operating table and little unfilled space. They emerged onto the upper deck and into a kind of hell, an inferno lit like day by bursting shells and searchlights beamed straight onto the *Castile* to bring her into sharp relief. Bullshit Shine came past, sweat-soaked, and paused when he saw the doctor.

'Mr Marty, sir. Hit bad I reckon.' He gestured for'ard. 'Save him if you can, Doctor. Old mate o' mine, one o' the bleeding best.' Bullshit Shine moved on, towards the after gun-batteries that were spitting out thunder and lightning. The ship shook like a dog as a near miss took the water close alongside and spray rose to cascade down over the decks. The din was unbelievable and Ommanney felt buffeted by it, buffeted almost out of his wits, his ability to think straight.

Followed by the LSBA he made for the fo'c'sle, keeping his feet with difficulty – there was blood on the steel deck. Marty in fact didn't take much seeing to. Ommanney bent down by his side. Scarcely any need to feel for a pulse but because it was the routine he did so. Half the gunner's head was stove in like a shattered coconut and there was a thick

120

segment of jagged steel sticking from his chest where it must have gone through the heart. 'Dead,' Ommanney said in a shaking voice. Death he had seen in plenty, but not in circumstances like these. 'Better get him below.'

'No point, sir. No 'ands either, not that can be spared in action. Leave him be. There's others still living.'

Ommanney nodded: true words! He went aft with his unused bag, leaving Marty's blood to drain over the side of the fo'c'sle.

ii

In Skegness, in the rooms that she'd kept on when Arthur had been appointed to the old *Castile*, Bess Marty had come sudddenly awake after a kind of nightmare and then couldn't get back to sleep so had got up and set the kettle on the gas ring in the sitting-room and made a cup of tea. Tea always helped. But Bess was worried and a little confused and she managed to knock a heavy brass ornament off a small table and it crashed to the floor with a thump. Then Bess dropped the cup of tea.

She sat down and cried.

A knock came at the door and it opened: the landlady, who lived below.

'Thought I heard a thump I did.'

'I – I'm ever so sorry, Mrs Gape.'

'That's all right. I couldn't sleep either. Must 'ave bin the welsh rabbit. Get indigestion something terrible I do, but what with the rationing. . . .' Mrs Gape, who 'did' for her lodgers and had cooked welsh rabbit for that night's supper, clicked her tongue. That Hitler had a lot to answer for and rationing was in Mrs Gape's view his most wicked sin. She had nobody at the war to worry about. Not this time; Gape, as she always referred to her late husband, had been in the last war, a driver in the RASC, and had died of peritonitis soon after demobilization, which Mrs Gape was in the habit of saying had saved the government having to pay her an army pension. She looked more closely at Bess.

121

'You're crying,' she announced.

'Y-yes. . . .'

'What's up?' Mrs Gape paused, eyes widening in concern. 'Is it your hubby? You've not had bad news, have you? Oh, I do 'ope – '

'No. It's not that. It's the worry, Mrs Gape.'

'Yes, I understand that. Look, I'll make some fresh tea, that lot's spoiled. Won't be a moment, Mrs Marty dear.' She went off with the teapot, to empty it in her own sink and brew the fresh lot. She was soon back with soothing words. 'Does no good to fret. But I know what worry is, my God I do! Used to worry meself sick about Gape I did, driving those army lorries and whatnot over there in France. Never 'ad a moment when I wasn't thinking of him. But in the end he come 'ome without a scratch. So will Mr Marty, you see.'

'Oh, how I hope so! We've been together – married anyway – so long. There's been absences, plenty of them, but you never get used to it. Not really.'

Mrs Gape nodded, pulled her dressing-gown around her, for the Lincolnshire night was sharp. 'Gape was only away for the war, not being a regular, so I don't really know. Before the war 'e drove a pantechnicon. 'Orses in them days. Never away for more than a night and that not often. Though I used to think I wouldn't mind if he was, not really. I don't know if you understand . . . Gape made a lot of work. Men do. I don't reckon they can 'elp it. Pipes an' that, and dirty feeders, dropping food round the table, dirty boots when they come in, you know the sort of thing, an' all the washing! Gape was pertickler about his underwear and 'e wore long pants down to the ankles, and thick vests, flannel. Gape was. . . .' Mrs Gape, as Bess recognized, was into her stride and wouldn't be stemmed. There was an earnest look on her heavy, not unkindly face as if she was determined to occupy Bess' mind and stop her worrying, a kind of personal war effort. Bess switched off, letting the verbiage flow. Mrs Gape seldom needed an answer. Bess

122

went on with her own thoughts. That sudden wakening: a sort of bang, or anyway a start, just as though something dreadful had happened and brought her awake. In the instant of waking she'd felt an enormous weight of fear that was succeeded by a most dreadful depression of spirit, as though nothing would ever come right again. That was still with her, and it had to do with Arthur.

She was convinced against all sane reason. that something had happened to him. If it had, then life would be over for her: she wouldn't want to go on. She sat in her chair motionless, rigid with worry. Mrs Gape's voice droned on and at last gave out. The landlady left with advice to Mrs Marty to go back to bed. But Bess sat on, waiting for the first of the day's BBC News broadcasts, to see if they said anything about the *Castile*.

iii

At about the time Cameron had brought his engines up to full, Evelyn Brown had arrived home in Fareham after a party in Southsea, a party that had gone on and on until the smuggled duty-free drink had been finished. The man, the army major of the previous night, had once again driven her home. He made to follow her in, proprietorially.

She stopped outside the front door. 'No, Andy. Not tonight. I'm sorry.'

The major's voice was slurred and angry. 'Why? I thought we – '

'I said no and I mean no.' There was a brittle sound, a verging on something like hysteria. She was fairly tight and very tired.

'Can't you tell me why, for God's sake? Is this an attack of conscience or something?'

A cold wind blew round her, coming off Portsmouth Harbour. She said, 'Perhaps. I don't know. Just leave me, Andy. I – I've got some thinking to do. You're not helping.'

'I see. So I'm just the poor bloody chauffeur, to be made use of – '

'No! I said I'm sorry.' She beat at him with soft fists in her frustration. 'Please *go*, Andy. I just don't want it tonight, that's all.'

He nodded knowingly. 'Wrong time of the month? You could have said before I – '

'It's not that.' She caught her breath. Stupid mistake: a ready-made excuse and she'd turned it up. Tears ran down her cheeks, visible as the major flicked a lighter to a cigarette.

'There's something more than just not wanting it, darling.'

'Yes, there is. Do you really want to know, Andy?'

'Well – '

She said, 'I've been suspecting . . . and today I went to the doctor. I'm bloody pregnant.'

'But that's – '

'I said I'm pregnant and I don't want – what you want. I – I can't really explain more than that.'

He laughed, a hard sound. 'Don't say you're going to pin it on me! Last night was the first goddam time – '

'Of course I'm not pinning it on you, don't be absurd. The point is, it could be my husband. *My husband's child.* Don't you *see*?'

'Not really,' the major answered sulkily.

'It's just that – that if it's John's child – '

'Not that you'd know.' The major laughed, a cynical sound. Then he apologized, for she might take a different line in a day or two's time. 'Shouldn't have said that, Eve.'

'No, you shouldn't. Look, you're married. Don't you know anything about women, the way they feel?'

'Not much. God knows I've tried with Susan, but – '

She said, 'Poor Susan,' and shut the door in his face. An oath came through and then she heard him going away. The car started up. She knew he thought she had turned into a prick-teaser. She didn't care. Men never did know anything about women, about their feelings, especially when pregnant – or preggers as the god-awful service slang had it.

124

The present generation that was, not her father's. Not that it wasn't far too soon to be pleading pregnancy as an excuse for having feelings, normally anyway. But this wasn't normal. It was true enough that she would never be sure whose child it was unless ultimately it showed some sort of likeness to the men in her recent life. Or to John, of course. And if it was John's, then for some obscure reason she didn't want it, even in its pre-embryonic stage, to be laid on by anyone else.

Fastidiousness? Or genuine conscience? Or just a funny feeling that for all she knew John might be facing danger? If so, then maybe that was conscience too. Unusually for her, she cried herself to sleep and woke feeling like hell, with a filthy hangover and horribly depressed. One thing was certain, and that was that whoever the father might be, her own father was to be presented with a grandchild. He would be pleased but with reservations: he thought a lot about his image, considering it youthful still. A grandchild would rock that particular boat. But her mother would be delighted, even relieved, at the bust image. Her father was a womanizer . . . Evelyn gave a tight grin: obviously, she took after him.

On that hungover awakening she, like Bess Marty a couple of hours earlier, listened, in her case desultorily, to the BBC News. Nothing much had been happening; a few Nazi bombers shot down over London, a few bombs dropped, some of them on Kent as the bombers retreated homeward. No British losses. There had been some activity in Northern Italy, the enemy had made a skirmish, his patrols probing southerly, and some prisoners had been taken. No mention of events at sea, no references to the *Castile*. Evelyn switched the set off; it hurt her head. In Skegness Bess Marty had given a sigh of relief and began to feel happier. Silly me, she thought, all that daft fuss, of course Arthur's going to be all right.

iv

The *Castile* moved on, silhouetted in the searchlights' glare,

125

beneath a hailstorm of fragmented steel. Cameron stood in the fore part of the bridge, staring ahead through his binoculars, looking for his target. Behind the binnacle Lieutenant Batten conned the ship on, giving frequent helm orders. He wished they could move ahead faster ; but that would be navigationally unwise. They couldn't risk jeopardizing the operation by piling the ship up before she reached the caisson across the entrance to the pens. Batten, however, believed they would never make it, that they hadn't a hope in hell. Someone at the Admiralty, or perhaps Winnie himself, had gone beyond reason, was expecting too much of a comparatively frail light cruiser without armoured sides. Already a shell had gone through the after flat – luckily without exploding, but it had left two holes in the ship's sides, port and starboard, and hadn't been far off the wardroom where the surgeon lieutenant was coping as best he could with upwards, at the last count, of twenty-nine casualties, many of them serious. Eight men plus Mr Marty had been killed, blown to fragments by the German artillery ashore. In the engine-room they were standing by for the last order, the order to get out, to leave in orderly fashion – they hoped – up the network of ladders and through the air-lock. Rogers, engineer officer in charge, would be the last to go, seeing all his black gang to safety first. That was the way with the navy.

On the flag deck Yeoman of Signals Robbins once again rubbed a hand along the initials he'd carved so many years ago in the wood of the guardrail. If Dorothy could see him now . . . but of course she could, looking down from aloft. Maybe she was waiting for him to join her, for the reunion. Once, soon after Dorothy had died, Robbins had read a book about death and the after life. He didn't know if he really believed what it said, but there was logic in it. When you passed over, you were assisted by helpers who were usually close relatives and these helpers took you in hand and acclimatized you to the new routine, the routine of heavenly peace under God the Captain, so that at the first

126

muster of the hands you'd not go and make a bollocks of it. Robbins' helpers would presumably be Dorothy and his long gone mum and dad, plus a sister lost in childhood. And any bloody minute now, Robbins thought as something whizzed over his head, which, had it not been bent a little over Dorothy's initials would have been taken off as if by a bacon slicer. He looked up, saw the great battle ensign that he'd hoisted on orders from the bridge a half-minute before the *Castile* had come between the arms of the breakwater. It waved in a stiffish breeze, a huge banner symbolizing the spirit of England. Scots and Irish too, of course, but to Yeoman of Signals Robbins, a southerner born and bred to the sounds and ambience of Pompey Town, England was more personal. *St George for Merrie England* . . . Robbins believed, searching his memory for a moment, that that rallying call had had some connection with the exploit of the old cruiser *Vindictive* at Zeebrugge, that last blockship business in 1918. He couldn't remember quite what it was.

'Yeoman!'

Cameron's voice. Robbins said, 'Yes, sir?' But no order came. Robbins had barely uttered when something happened above his head. The Nazi gunfire had taken the foretopmast and with it the director and its crew. Tackle fell to the flag deck, a tangle of twisted metal and radar and WT aerials. Robbins, flinging himself at the rush across to starboard, just about missed it. He looked in horror: amongst the shatter and twist there were bodies, mangled and bleeding, and one of them still alive was shrieking on a high note of agony and fear. The mast itself was hanging over the side, held by a wire guy to trail down into the water of the harbour. After a moment Robbins realized he hadn't escaped entirely: something had hit him on the way down to the flag deck and his left arm was numb, useless. With his right hand he felt himself for further damage but couldn't find any. He was certainly alive; Dorothy wasn't ready for him yet.

Cameron's voice came again. 'Are you all right, Yeoman?'

'Yes, sir, fighting fit, sir.' You didn't bleat about a numb arm with the ship in action. The doc would have plenty to do now as if he hadn't already. For some curious reason, doubtless to do with the tangle all around him, Robbins' mind went back to his earlier commission in the old *Castile*. Singapore, and a fracas in the naval canteen ashore. A rating from the *Castile* had got into an argument with a stoker from another ship. Nobody except the two men immediately concerned had any idea what the argument was all about, but within a couple of minutes the fighting had become general, all the *Castiles* piling into the other ship's company and the men from ships not primarily concerned taking sides, not wanting to be left out. There had been total pandemonium. Chairs were lifted and brought down on heads. Glass flew everywhere, bottles of Brickwood's beer – it was astonishing how Brickwood's got around the Empire – smashed and discharged their contents and blood flowed freely from cuts and gashes. Limp bodies all over the show, Robbins remembered, fists swung at jaws, windows and tables and bar fittings smashed. The naval shore patrol had come in, the PO had taken a look and at once retreated to send urgent signals for reinforcements. Aboard the ships in the port guards had been hastily fallen in and despatched ashore, belted and with side-arms. The fighting had spilled over from the canteen into the dockyard itself and the master-at-arms of the flagship of the light cruiser squadron had been seized and lifted and passed overhead from one man to another and dumped in the water.

There had been a real stink afterwards. All shore leave had been stopped and the squadron had gone to sea, cutting short its stay. Those arrested as ringleaders had been taken out of their ships to remain in Singapore for the court of enquiry and then the courts martial. The rating from the *Castile* had been sent back in cells to UK to serve ninety days' detention in the Pompey Detention Quarters and, curiously perhaps to those who didn't understand the navy, the *Castile* had basked in a degree of glory: the lads had put up a memorable fight and no-one in their senses liked masters-at-arms.

The *Castile* was going to put up another good fight now, her very last. As she moved on with her guns firing to port and starboard and ahead, like some great firework, Bullshit Shine could be seen yelling encouragement at the guns' crews. With the director gone, the ship was now in gunlayers' firing, each gun blasting away independently as they came in closer to the target. Ordinary Seaman Quentin, shaking like a leaf, moved back from his gun, moved into the lee of the bridge superstructure which acted as a kind of splinter screen.

He was spotted by the chief gunner's mate.

'You, there. *Skulking.*'

Quentin didn't utter; he just stood there, staring wide-eyed at Bullshit Shine. Shine said, 'Ship's in action, lad, as if you didn't know. Back to your gun. Or else.'

The voice was hard, shouting above the thunder of the batteries and the rattle, now, of close-range weapons. The face was if anything harder. Quentin went back, took up his position as part of the gun's crew. Naval discipline, Royal Naval discipline, was perhaps the toughest in the world, and was deeply inculcated from the day you joined as a new entry; and it held when the chips were down. It held because you were more scared of the Captain than of the enemy, and in certain circumstances such as now the chief gunner's mate represented the authority of the Captain and you were scared of him too.

Shine came up behind him and shouted in his ear. 'Hold fast, lad. It won't go on for ever.'

Quentin nodded. He felt totally dazed by the terrible din, by the gun flashes, by the probing searchlight beams that when they lit upon him seemed to burn into him and display his inner terror of the whole situation, and to make him a

129

personal target for Hitler and the killers of the Third Reich. He felt Shine's heavy hand come down on his shoulder, a friendly hand somewhat surprisingly. 'You'll be all right,' Bullshit Shine said. Again Quentin nodded and found himself thinking of his old tutor at King's. That dry old man had said sailors were Philistines, a rough, common lot. But the rough hand of Chief PO Shine had comfort in it, comfort and confidence, a feeling of solidity, a part of the real world beyond the colleges of Cambridge and their fusty bookshelves, sherry in the senior common room as the old men made their obscure, learned jokes in Latin or Greek or spoke disparagingly of colleagues behind their backs. When men like Shine had criticism to offer, they said it to your face. Quentin had learned that much.

v

Ahead beyond the turn that soon the *Castile* would make to starboard for her final run in, a group of fighters from the Resistance waited in a cellar beneath a small café alongside the old ferry terminal. The café was called, or had been called, the Brighton Bar, but the name on the fascia had been painted out by the Nazis who had not bothered to rename it. Neither had the proprietor, old Jean-Paul Cuvillier, bothered. One day the war would end and the stinking Bosch would go and then the Brighton Bar would re-emerge to welcome day trippers from England's south coast. Jean-Paul Cuvillier would wait: he was old, but not that old, and he knew the Allies were going to win the war. Winston Churchill himself had said as much, and what Winston Churchill said was always the truth. No-one doubted that in Occupied France.

The group of seven sat in silence, listening to the sounds from outside. They were all smoking Gauloise cigarettes and the air was thick. One of them was a girl, though dressed as a man in blue jersey and beret and thick rough trousers. The men, five of them French, one of them

English, wore German uniforms, those of infantry soldiers of the Reich. Beneath the beret the girl's hair was cut short, very short; only now starting to grow properly again. She had been accused of collaboration and had had her head shaved to become an object of scorn for patriotic Frenchmen and women. This was acceptable to her; she was no collaborator, but it did no harm for the Nazis to see her as such. She had learned a good deal from the Nazi officers who had wined and dined her and gone to bed with her afterwards and what she had learned had been passed on and had eventually reached the War Cabinet in London. She was much honoured; she was the Comtesse de Perpignan, but was known simply as Marie, which was nicely nondescript. When the beret was off and when her hair grew again, she would be seen to be pretty.

It was she who spoke. She spoke to the Englishman sitting a little apart from the others. This was the agent to be picked up.

'You will not forget the messages? The personal messages.'

'I'll not forget, Marie. Though I wish – ' He broke off.

'You wish?'

The Englishman made a gesture of negation. 'It doesn't matter.' It did, of course; but time was short and it was too late to say again what he had said already. Marie's messages were for a major of Intelligence serving at the War office in London, the very man to whom the Englishman was to report in his official capacity. Marie had known the major from pre-war days when she had paid many visits to London; her messages were ones of love, and the Englishman, who had come to know Marie well, was jealous. He loved her; he had no wish to return to England but war was war, duty was duty, and he was badly needed.

Marie said, 'Now it will not be long, I think.'

The sounds were coming closer, the terrible din of the gunfire. Heavy vehicles rumbled past the café, shaking even the cellar: tanks, probably, bringing more guns to bear on the British ship. As a short lull came, they all heard shouted orders from outside, and then a blast on a whistle. Immediately after this, the firing was resumed and seemed even heavier than before.

The leader of the group stood up. 'The signal,' he said, referring to the whistle. 'Now we stand by. If all has gone well, Pierre will knock at the café door.'

He moved to the foot of the stone steps leading up from the cellar. The others followed, the Englishman now in the centre. As they reached the top of the steps there was a very heavy explosion from the direction of the pens, and the cellar rocked, pieces of stone and plaster flaking down from the walls.

11

ON THE BRIDGE Cameron staggered backwards, to be brought up short by the binnacle that seemed to have a life of its own, kicking him in the back like a horse. Hugh Batten, the navigator, was flat on his back. Cameron gave him a hand up. He said, 'Well, we made it, sir.'

'Thanks to you. Well done, Pilot.'

Batten didn't respond. It had been a team effort – guns, engines, quartermaster, himself as navigating officer, Cameron as the skipper who would take the blame if anything went wrong. Which it still could even though the old ship had been nicely positioned, slap against the caisson when the bows had driven in hard and the explosives had gone up as planned. The caisson and the dockside, the entry to the pens, had been shattered and fires were burning. In the light of those fires the commandos could be seen : they had jumped for the dockside on the heels of the explosion and now they were advancing slowly behind their sub machine-guns towards the Nazi port defences, the skirl of the pipes sounding bravely out until they were submerged in the din of the battle.

'Abandon, sir ?'

Cameron said, 'No, not yet. We're better where we are till *Dionysus* comes in.' The engine-room had been cleared of all hands just one minute before the ship had hit ; the engines had been left on full ahead and the evacuation had been orderly, no accidents due to haste. Below decks aft, Chief Stoker Rump looked around: he and his black gang, plus the engine-room tiffies and the engineer officer himself, were packed into the wardroom flat, the pantry, and the officers' cabins and other spaces, along with such seamen as were not engaged as guns' crews. There was a stink of ether and antiseptics from the wardroom itself, where the doctor was more than fully occupied, seeing to the preparations for getting the wounded men away when the order came from the bridge, no easy task. Jimmy the One was with him, Rump saw, another old *Castile* hand to be present as the ship died.

She was dying now: she wouldn't last long, Rump knew from the feel of her, broken for'ard and taking water fast. Soon she would settle in her blockship position, main deck awash. It was a sad day. Rump said as much to Chief Petty Officer Barker, now down from the wheelhouse. No-one was needed to steer a ship in the *Castile*'s predicament.

'Not that sad, Rump,' Barker said, wiping sweat from his face. 'She had to go sometime. Like all of us, eh? And she'll be remembered even if we aren't. It's not a bad way to go, all said an' done.'

'They grow not old, as we that are left grow old,' Rump quoted.

'Don't bloody speak too soon,' Barker said. 'We're still in a perishin' mess.' He watched the First Lieutenant going past, making for the ladder to the upper deck, and envied him the freedom of the fresh air. The orders were that the ship's company were to remain below for their own safety but Barker knew that if the Nazis started shelling again – and for some reason or other they were not currently firing on the ship, perhaps because they were now more concerned about the commandos – they could be caught like rats in a trap. Cameron's decision would release them and that wouldn't come until the skipper was in all respects ready to order a withdrawal. Some hope, Barker thought bitterly: they were all due, if they lived, to finish the war in Hitler's Germany, in a POW camp. That stood out a mile.

The First Lieutenant reached the bridge, reported to Cameron. 'All hands below, sir. Ready and waiting.'

'Casualties?'

'Only a rough count so far. Forty-three wounded, fifteen dead.'

'Boats?'

'One whaler serviceable, sir. The rest are smashed. I've already had the whaler swung out and – ' John Brown broke off as a shout came from Robbins on the flag deck.

'*Dionysus* moving in now, sir!'

Cameron swung his binoculars. 'Rather too soon,' he said. Hell had returned to the outer channel: gunfire, heavy stuff, from ship to shore, searchlights, the glare of fires, and above it all what the yeoman had recognized, the destroyer's foretopmast moving in beneath her battle ensign. Cameron turned to Brown. 'Right, Number One. Lowerers to stand by the whaler, prepare to embark casualties.'

'Aye, aye, sir.' Brown made for the ladder down to the upper deck. He knew the main disembarkation would have to wait for the commandos. He didn't really expect to get anyone away in safety. The Admiralty might have done better, he thought, to have sent in a hospital ship rather than a destroyer. The Nazis just might have respected her red crosses. Might, but probably wouldn't. No reason why they should, really, in the circumstances. He probably wouldn't himself. They were all at war, after all, and the Nazis were being given a very bloody nose. Making his way towards the whaler's falls, Brown witnessed what he considered a curious and revealing incident. One of the ordinary seamen, his shoulders shaking, was coming up from the wardroom hatch with what looked like a sheet, no doubt from one of the officers' cabins. The man was moving fast, eyes staring, and he started to wave the sheet. As a reflex action Brown jerked his revolver from its holster

135

round his waist: Cameron had ordered all officers, before the light cruiser had entered the port, to arm themselves. And Brown would have shot any man who showed surrender to the Nazis. He didn't need to, however: behind the rating came another OD: MacTavish. MacTavish grabbed the man from behind and snatched the sheet away. He started shouting, something about yellow bastards – there was too much noise in the port to hear more than that – and then he put the man out with a smashing blow to the jaw.

John Brown re-stowed his revolver. Well, well. You never knew . . . and action often brought out the best. It was a pity MacTavish still faced that charge.

ii

In Bodmin after the dawn was up, Mary Anne Blake had as yet no means of knowing she was a war widow now. Her mother, Mrs Larkspur, unable to get back to sleep after a fraught night, came to Mary Anne's room early, with a tray.

'Tea, dear.'

'Thanks, mum.'

Mrs Larkspur smiled in relief: the girl sounded much better. Daylight always calmed fears. 'It's a nice morning,' she said. 'Sunny for a wonder. All that rain !' That was the trouble with the West Country, of course, it rained all the time, day after day, sometimes week after week, as the lows and whatnot swept in from the Atlantic. Of course, the BBC didn't give weather reports, not in wartime, in case the Germans got to hear and were given assistance in plotting their air raids ; but when you'd lived long enough in the West Country you knew without being told that it was going to rain, and blow too more often than not.

But not today: it looked set fair, more or less, and that would be a help. They might all go out somewhere, walk on the moor perhaps, or go on the bus to Camelford. She made the suggestion.

'All right, mum.' Mary Anne drank her tea while Mrs Larkspur, drawing back the curtains first, sat on the bed. 'Anything on the News?'

'Not yet, dear. I mean, it's early.'

'I've been thinking of Peter.'

'I know, dear – '

'I hope he's all right.'

'Oh, I'm sure he is.' Mrs Larkspur gave a confident smile. 'He's in a nice big ship – '

'Not all that big. He never seemed really happy about this appointment, mum, you know that.'

'Well, perhaps not, dear, but that's no evidence of anything at all, is it? Lots of people don't like what they have to do. Your father for one. He didn't like being in the army in the last war. Right from the time we met he used to say he'd been given all the worst jobs.' The then Lieutenant Larkspur had been in the Ordnance, in France, and sometimes quite close to the trenches. 'But he came back, didn't he? Safe and sound as a bell.'

'Yes . . .' Soon after this the BBC News came on to be received in every home in the land and listened to in pregnant silence, senses strained to try and catch and interpret every nuance in the voice of Bruce Belfrage, or Gordon MacLeod, or Alvar Lidell. But no mention of the *Castile*, as noted, among the others, by Bess Marty and Evelyn Brown in their own parts of Britain.

Another listener was Rosie Shine, in Rowlands Castle, who went for an early walk, before breakfast but after the News, down Redhill Road to the Green, exercising the dog. Two years old, he was a bulldog and the name had suggested itself: Winston. He already had a middle-aged look, sturdy and staid except when he saw a cat and then all hell was let loose. He saw a cat this morning, moving with lifted tail towards Links Lane. Winston was after it in a flash, barking on a high, excited note. No use calling him, though for form's sake Rosie Shine did. Somebody must love that cat. Sighing, she altered course and followed up

137

Links Lane where there were big houses, largely inhabited by naval officers, retired and too old to be recalled for service.

Down Links Lane now came one of them, Captain Hartley, old enough to have served in the sail training squadron long since gone.

He took off his hat. 'Morning, Mrs Shine.'

'Good morning, Captain Hartley.' They stopped for a chat; the old man was lonely, a widower, and was always friendly.

'Any news of your husband, Mrs Shine?'

'No. . . .'

'Oh well. No news is good news as they say. I'll not ask you where he is, where the old *Castile* is – '

'I wouldn't know,' she cut in.'

'Of course not. But I'll make a guess: convoy escort. They're the ones who're going to win this war, Mrs Shine. Without 'em we'd starve inside a week, so they say. I believe 'em.' The old man lifted his walking stick and aimed it in a south-easterly direction. 'Queer to think those damn Nazi fellers are just over there and daren't come any closer. Wish I could get at the buggers.' He seemed unaware of his language. 'It's hateful to be old in time of war, Mrs Shine. I keep in touch vicariously through my boy, and that's about all.' Rosie Shine knew that Hartley's son was captain of a battle-cruiser, but the old man always referred to him as his boy. She didn't know that when the admiral had lifted and aimed his stick, he had pointed it by sheer chance directly at the caisson in which the shattered forepart of the *Castile* lay embedded and embattled.

iii

The man referred to as Pierre had given his knock at the door of the café in Dieppe and had then waited as from time to time the flickering fires in the port threw him into silhouette. He was a young man, thick-set, wearing a long

138

black leather topcoat and a trilby hat. He could have been, and in fact was intended to be, taken for an officer of the Gestapo. His German was flawless.

He waited. No-one was taking any notice of him. Nazi units moved past, infantry and armour. Not in fact a large concentration: so many Germans had been withdrawn from the area and sent to ports believed by their High Command to be under more immediate threat from the British. Pierre grinned to himself: the local Resistance had helped in that, passing and receiving information from London and laying many a red herring in the right quarters to confuse the Bosch and speed him on his useless way.

The door opened, and the elderly *maquis* leader stood there. There was no light behind him.

'Now,' Pierre said.

'It is safe to move?'

'As safe as ever it will be, Jean-Paul. The British commandos are now on the jetty. We must take our chance.'

'So be it, then.' Jean-Paul Cuvillier stood aside, and spoke to the German-uniformed men and the woman in rear. The Englishman came forward and put his hands on his shoulders.

'Thank you for all you've done, you and all your friends. You're a very gallant company, m'sieur.'

Cuvillier shrugged. 'It is nothing, it is our duty as patriotic Frenchmen. You yourself are a brave man, m'sieur. May God go with you this day.'

Nothing more was said. The Englishman left the café with the five men, turning to the right towards the centre of the town. The girl Marie, Comtesse de Perpignan, also left the café but made in the opposite direction, hurrying, though not quite running: to run would look suspicious perhaps and no risks must be taken. It was a risk being out in the streets at all: most of the town's inhabitants would be keeping their heads down while the sounds of the fighting continued. But it would have been more of a risk to have

139

remained in the café or the cellar. The Germans had their avenues of intelligence too, and there were always traitors. Experience had taught that always it was only a matter of time before a Resistance cell was tracked down, and the time of the café had come to an end with the departure from it of the English agent. Only Jean-Paul Cuvillier remained, since it was his café and to disappear would of itself look suspicious to the Nazis.

The girl vanished round a corner.

Behind Pierre the five Resistance men with their valuable guest turned to the left before reaching the town's main shopping street, following the line of the railway track that led to Rouen and Paris as it curved around the perimeter of the port. Certain arrangements had been made with the Special Operations Executive in London, very detailed arrangements that had been imprinted on the minds of the local Resistance men and on the minds of the British commandos now fighting through behind their sub machine-guns and the solitary piper, playing still. A rendezvous had been agreed behind a warehouse close to a bridge that spanned the railway line. This was where the commandos were making for. When they reached their objective one of the Resistance men would identify his party by two long and two short flashes from a torch. Then the commandos would fight back towards the *Castile* and a pick-up by the incoming destroyer. The timing would have to be exactly right; and they were going to need a good deal of luck.

iv

Chief Petty Officer Froggett, chief bosun's mate, stood by the falls of the whaler that awaited Cameron's order for embarkation and slipping. Now the destroyer was not far off. Her guns were keeping up a continuous bombardment of the port installations, and no-one seemed to be firing back at her. Froggett fancied the Jerries had been caught well and truly on the hop, their pants right down around their ankles. He wondered, as he awaited the final orders from the bridge, what it would be like if Hitler ever decided to mount an operation against Pompey dockyard. Of course, he would never get there. Those old sea forts that dotted Spithead would presumably go into action for the first time since they had been built nearly a hundred years before, by Lord Palmerston, to keep the French out if they had gone to war and invaded them – and the other port defences. Pompey wouldn't be caught napping. Or would it? Often enough the brass wasn't all that clever and often, too, there was a high degree of complacency on the part of admirals. Froggett had once been coxswain of the admiral's barge in the Home Fleet flagship, the *Rodney* at that time. They'd been at Invergordon on the Cromarty Firth and the admiral had been complacent about the weather despite Froggett's respectful warning that a blow was in the offing. He had left it a shade too long in coming off shore from a courtesy call upon the Provost of Nairn. There had been a lot of tooth-sucking and muttering from the barge's crew and in the upshot they'd nearly capsized coming back across the Moray Firth. It had been Froggett's seamanship that had saved the day, and saved the admiral too. But the admiral hadn't appeared to notice: he was too full of whisky and Froggett had received no thanks at all, only an admonition for an uncomfortable trip back. He remembered now, with a chuckle, that the Flag Lieutenant had looked a nice shade of green . . . the battleship navy didn't get a lot of real sea time in, spending most of the time either alongside the South Railway jetty in Pompey, or swinging round a buoy somewhere.

Pompey.

As the land battle waged along the jetty and the men of the *Castile* waited for the commandos to return with their prize, Froggett, whose home was in North End in Pompey town, thought back to his recall to active service after five years of pension and the beach. It had been grand to be back in uniform again, to walk into RNB in Queen Street and be recognized as a man of importance, a chief petty officer. He remembered the time Neville Chamberlain had gone to Munich in 1938 to appease the German Chancellor when war had seemed on the cards. Froggett had been recalled then too, and the gas masks had appeared on the streets of Portsmouth, worn by the libertymen ashore and in the barracks too. It had been a stirring time for an old sailor who remembered the previous war and Froggett had been somewhat chokker at being stood down again soon after Chamberlain had come back waving a piece of paper and an umbrella.

'Peace in our time,' he'd said, giving a yellow-toothed smile from beneath his moustache.

Bollocks had been Chief PO Froggett's reaction: you could never trust Hitler. They ought to have had Winnie at the helm. He'd have stopped Hitler in his tracks without even having to go to war to do it. Froggett wasn't desperately keen on war as such; he had no wish to see men die or to die himself come to that. But he loved the comradeship of the service, the swopping of yarns of old commissions, the going ashore in strange ports, the sense of belonging to something very special.

Also it had been nice to be away from his wife. Ethel, he had to admit, bored him stiff. She was lumpish and cowlike and seldom spoke, opening her mouth chiefly to eat, which she did a lot of and looked like it. Cottage loaf shaped, was Ethel, sitting about the small terraced house as though she was on a shelf in a baker's shop, getting staler. He'd had to go home to her, once again demobbed, once again on a small pension eked out by his job as a bank messenger. When he came in and gave her the news, she sent him down to the Home and Colonial for some groceries. A year later, however, it had come for real and Froggett was back again in the Andrew. He remembered the thrill, almost as if he'd been joining for the first time, but with a difference because he had those vivid memories of the last lot and now his

142

youth was being brought back to him and the fleet was gearing up in a manner that it hadn't done since 1914. All those years of neglect and disarmament, of ships being scrapped or relegated to the Reserve Fleet, of officers and men themselves being axed, put on the scrapheap before their due time . . . all that was over for the duration, everything was going the other way. Froggett recalled being on a Corporation trolley-bus going from the Circle in Southsea to Portsmouth Hard and the dockyard's Main Gate. Outside the Queen's Hotel in Osborne Road a crowd of young RNVR sub-lieutenants had boarded and the sight of all those wavy stripes had brought the past back strongly. Wars apart, you didn't see much of wavy stripes or of the interlaced stripes of the professional seamen from the Merchant Service, the RNR officers. They'd got off outside the *Vernon*, the torpedo establishment, talking like schoolboys, keen to get on with the job. Froggett had gone on to the Hard and walked through the Main Gate of the dockyard, walked past great peacetime liners being converted into armed merchant cruisers destined for the Northern Patrol or to act as convoy escorts to eke out the destroyers of which there were never to be enough. The *Monarch of Bermuda*, *Queen of Bermuda*, *Asturias*, *Alcantara* . . . all the peacetime luxury fittings being ripped out by the dockyard mateys in many yards besides Pompey to make room for the austerity of messdecks to accommodate the naval crews and the guns and the ammunition spaces. To Froggett there was a kind of romance in it all, getting ready for a real job, the tinsel glitter gone.

Then, anyway. Soon enough this war had turned into horror, much more so than in the last one. There had been a kind of chivalry then and often the U-boat commanders had seen to it that the merchant crews got away in the boats before firing off the tin fish to sink the ships. Not any more. And there had been scant romance in the sinking of the *Athenia* soon after September 3, 1939. All those children aboard. . . .

12

THE WHALER WAS filled to capacity with stretcher cases, men immobilized in the Neil Robertson stretchers that permitted rough handling, lowering and hoisting and so on, without risk of injury or further pain. The lowerers were ready at the falls; Leading Seaman Pafford was already embarked to take charge of the trip across to the *Dionysus*; with him was the LSBA who would be responsible for the wounded men. The doctor was remaining aboard in case of further need. The doctor in the *Dionysus* would take over his patients for the time being. Lieutenant(E) Rogers with his engine-room ratings was standing by aft to jump over and swim to the destroyer; the need for them aboard the *Castile* had come to an end now. All other officers and all seamen ratings would remain aboard until Cameron passed the word to abandon ship.

Froggett died at 0236, when a stray bullet from the shore passed through his head, less than a minute after the laden whaler had been lowered and slipped to be pulled across to the destroyer.

ii

The skirl of the pipes had stopped. Cameron, watching through binoculars, had seen the piper fall, had seen tracer cut the man's body like a scythe. He had been picked up by a big corporal of marines and carried into the lee of a warehouse. When the corporal realized the man was dead, he left him on the cobbles of the dock and rejoined the rest of the commandos. The body would be picked up on the way back to the ship. Soon after Cameron had seen the incident a swirl of red-tinged smoke swept across from one of the fires started by the naval bombardment, and he lost sight of the action.

He looked at his watch: time was passing too fast, by now the commando force should have made its contact with the Resistance. Then he saw some of the marines coming back through the smoke and flame, moving backwards, keeping up their fire as they came, attempting in fact to move forward again when the Nazi fire temporarily slackened.

'I don't like the look of it,' Batten said.

'Nor me, Pilot. It's a retreat if you ask me.'

As Cameron watched in growing concern, he saw two more men go down, caught in the Nazi gunfire. They fell in spreading pools of blood as their comrades kept up the running fight, firing back into the swirling smoke.

Batten said, 'They need help, sir.'

'That's what I was thinking.' Cameron leaned over the after screen of the bridge and shouted down. 'Chief gunner's mate!'

A figure emerged from the lee of the funnel casing. 'Sir?'

'Landing parties,' Cameron called. 'Issue rifles, Chief, fast as you can, then fall in all seamen and stokers along the waist, starboard side.'

'Aye, aye, sir!' Chief PO Shine doubled aft, slithering from time to time in patches of blood. He contacted CPO Barker, acting buffer in place of Froggett, and Chief Stoker Rump, and passed the word: even in the heat of battle it was etiquette to let the chief stoker detail his own men after formal consultation with the engineer officer. Then Bullshit Shine moved down to the wardroom flat where the keyboard sentry was already releasing the chains from the trigger guards of the racked rifles: you didn't leave

145

weapons for enemy use and the rifles would have been dumped in the harbour waters before the *Castile* was abandoned. 'Issue 'em out, lad,' Shine ordered. 'And smack it about – up to the waist – I'll give you a hand.'

Back on deck, Chief PO Barker was being sceptical of landing parties. 'Don't know that we'll be all that much bleedin' help! You know the old story of the parade ground, eh? Royal Marines will advance in column of fours, seamen will advance in bloody great 'eaps.' Seamen didn't look at things in quite the same way as the spit-and-polish brigade. But Barker didn't say this in Bullshit Shine's hearing.

ii

A man in a shiny black leather topcoat, not the man François but a genuine officer of the hated Gestapo, knocked at the door of the café where Jean-Paul Cuvillier had remained behind alone. With the Gestapo man was a squad of uniformed storm troopers from the *Waffen* SS, élite of the Party's rank and file. More men, not in view from the front of the café, were in position to watch all likely exits.

There was an answer to the knock, somewhat to the Gestapo man's surprise. Cuvillier stood there, calm, collected and indignant.

'At this hour, to disturb a man asleep?' Cuvillier was wearing an old-fashioned nightshirt and carried a candle in an enamelled holder, plate-like. Only the nightcap was missing from what was a Dickensian scene. 'What is the meaning of – '

The Gestapo man brought up a revolver. 'Inside, old man, or I shall shoot.'

Cuvillier stepped backwards, staring at the Gestapo man, who followed him into the café, the revolver pressed into Cuvillier's stomach. The SS contingent remained on guard at the exit. The questioning began.

146

'Where is the Englishman?'

'I don't know what you're talking about – '

'You know very well, Cuvillier. You have been watched. I ask again, where is the Englishman?'

'I say again, I know of no Englishman.'

A hand came up, snakelike in its speed, and its bony back took Cuvillier across each cheek in succession, twice. Weals appeared, and blood, from a heavy gold ring. 'You will speak or there will be much pain.'

'I have nothing to say. Except this. You are swine, you Nazis, dirty pigs, murderers and rapists and plunderers. And you are not going to win the war.'

The Gestapo man gave an icy smile, staring back into Cuvillier's eyes. 'You are foolish to say these things, Cuvillier. But also brave. Brave when it comes to yourself. I wonder if you are so brave when it comes to other people. What do you think, Cuvillier?'

'I think nothing. You speak in riddles.'

The Gestapo man's smile was still there, still icy, and his next words came softly. 'We have the woman, Cuvillier. We have Madame la Comtesse de Perpignan, known as Marie. She is very beautiful, as you know.'

'I do not know her, *cochon*.'

'Oh, but I know you do! I tell you again, Cuvillier, you and your Resistance people have been watched. You will take me to the Englishman, at once.'

Cuvillier looked down towards his feet, hiding the sudden gleam that had come to his eyes. It was obvious that the Gestapo man spoke at least some of the truth; Cuvillier had known that the Nazis were on his trail. But it was also obvious that they had finally moved in just too late and still believed that the Englishman was hidden away, possibly even now not seeing a connection between the Englishman and the British ships that had come into the port. Very well, then: he, Cuvillier, could still be of some use. He could delay.

He said, 'There is no Englishman. You have been misled.'

147

'I shall search. You will keep close to me. I – '

The pretence was best kept up as long as possible. 'You have no right to enter my premises, nor to search, and I – '

'I have the right. I represent the conquering power. You are nothing but a dirty Frenchman. Even your Allies the British call you frogs. Now turn around, my friend Cuvillier.' The Nazi gave a signal to the SS men. Two of them remained to guard the door, two others entered the café and closed in on Cuvillier. The girl was not present. Cuvillier wondered: he believed that part of it was bluff, that Marie had managed to vanish, at any rate for the time being.

iii

The First Lieutenant reported to the bridge.

'Landing parties ready, sir.'

'Right, Number One. Split 'em in two, you take one, Calcott the other. You've seen the area on the plans – have you got your bearings?'

Brown nodded.

'Right, fine. You take the right of the warehouse, Calcott's lot the left. Pincer movement. At the very least, you should cause something of a diversion.'

Brown nodded again. For diversion, he thought, read cannon fodder, but no doubt it all helped. He believed it was daft but saw that Cameron had little option. They couldn't go back – if go back they ever did – to Portsmouth and say they'd achieved half the objective of the mission and had then left the commandos to fry and the agent to fall into Nazi hands. They would have a damn good go and if they failed, then they failed. Brown, in any case, felt he had little to live for: that anonymous letter was heavy on his mind.

He went fast down the ladder from the bridge, sliding the rails through his hands, feet barely touching the steps. In the waist Calcott was waiting. 'All right, Sub?' Brown asked.

'I'll be all right.'

'Course you will.' Brown passed Cameron's orders. The din was appalling now, everything in the port seeming to be firing. The *Dionysus* was keeping it up well, her shells landing with good effect, but the commandos themselves were still pinned down. Behind the First Lieutenant the men of the landing parties began jumping for the jetty, Calcott landing in a heap but picking himself up quickly. Seamen and stokers were all together now, branch distinctions forgotten. Chief Stoker Rump, breathing heavily, knowing that he was leaving the ship for good and all since the landing parties wouldn't be re-boarding, pounded on in rear of the First Lieutenant. There was no time to dwell on the past, not really, but Rump did dwell on certain aspects because he believed he was going to die, that none of them could hope to survive the bullets, and death was a serious business, the departure from life itself being more momentous than leaving a ship for the last time. Rump was praying that his many sins, which were mostly of a womanizing nature, might be forgiven. Or if not forgiven, quite, then overlooked. It hadn't been all his fault ; who but God himself put desires into the minds of men ? Rump was only human, albeit frail when it came to temptation. He recalled that night in Pompey when he'd joined the *Castile* for the second time, that woman in Queen Street. It was true he hadn't gone with her in the end but that had nothing to do with the resistance of temptation; shortage of money more like. So God wouldn't be chalking up anything there in his favour. Another point: if there had been any women in Scapa, he'd have had another try.

There had been so many: Hong Kong, Singapore, Colombo, Sydney, Wellington, Bermuda, Malta, Gibraltar, Cape Town as well as the home ports, each landmark of a seafaring life carrying its female associations. By no means all prozzies : they had been the port in the storm, to be turned to when Rump hadn't been in a particular port for long enough to make proper contacts. You didn't need to

149

chat up prozzies, no need to get the charm to work. As a young man Rump had been full of charm, or so many girls had thought, and he often wondered how many little Rumps were making their way in the world. Not too many, he hoped: that wouldn't go down at all well up aloft. And of course there was his wife in Newcastle . . . but she was unlikely to find out, of course; he hoped she never would, not wishing to hurt her after he had gone.

Rump, bending low, advanced along the jetty behind the First Lieutenant, praying harder than ever as the bullets came close. He felt a graze, something nicking his left shoulder, but it wasn't much and he carried on. Ahead of the line of advance, slap between the naval landing parties and the commandos, there was a heavy explosion that sent chunks of concrete flying. Rump swore viciously: that looked like a projy from the destroyer.

'Daft prats,' he said to no-one in particular. Not nice, if you were rubbed out by your own side.

iv

In London, in an imposing room in a quiet, tall house in Knightsbridge, a group of men wearing plain clothes sat round a highly polished mahogany table. They had been discussing the latest report from the undercover radio transmitter in Dieppe and there had been a good deal of cross-comment.

'Not going all in our favour – '

'The pens appear to be blocked, old boy.'

'Yes, that's one half of the mission. But in my view it's a damn sight more important to get Frank out.'

'Oh, I agree, if the Nazis – '

'If the Nazis get him we're set to lose a whole underground network – '

'If he talks. I'm certain he won't.'

'Every man has his breaking point under torture, Stephen. So for that matter has a woman.'

150

An eye was cocked. 'You're thinking of Marie?'

'Of course. What did that report say?' He answered his own question. 'Cuvillier's cell has been rumbled – '

'But he reported he'd got Frank away, remember.'

'Yes, and just in time by the sound of it. He also reported that Marie had left the café . . . and that other business.'

'Frank?'

'That Cuvillier suspects he's gone soft on Marie, yes. I don't like it. If he's worried about her, he could refuse to leave.'

'Not a chance. Frank's too professional. Besides, he'd never slip the escort. They have orders to bring him to UK and that's that.' The speaker looked around the table, then at his watch. 'Anything else? I'm due at Number Ten – '

'There's the commandos themselves, and the ships' companies. Cuvillier's report said there's very heavy fighting.'

'Out of our control, old boy. I always thought the operation wasn't being given enough back-up, but it's a trifle too late now, isn't it? We really can't worry about the navy, it's Frank, that's all.'

'But for God's sake . . . the navy's there to get him out! If they – '

'Taken care of, old boy, taken care of. We all know Frank's importance, but it lies mostly in not allowing the Nazis to get him. Rather than in his intrinsic value, you see. So if he's killed in the fighting, it's just too bad – both for us and for the Nazis.'

'But if he's taken alive?'

'He won't be, old boy, he won't be.' There was a pause. 'The officer commanding the marines has those orders – to bring Frank to UK. Dead or alive. I'm sure you understand.'

There seemed to be nothing further to say. It was now a case of waiting. It was going to be a long night. There were yawns; coffee was brought by an old man in waiter's rig, starched shirt, wing collar, black tail coat. Thoughts drifted

151

to mundane matters, personal matters. Golf, wives, lady friends, week-ends in the country. Life wasn't all war. Not a great deal of thought was spared for the ships' companies engaged in Dieppe. After all, as had been said, everything was taken care of.

Across the Channel in Dieppe, other matters were being taken care off, matters that the Special Operations Executive in London were not yet aware of. Jean-Paul Culliver's radio had gone into action, very briefly, before the Gestapo's arrival at the café. Once the Gestapo had come, there had to be silence. Thereafter the search of the café and the cellar was thorough. Naturally no Englishman was found, but the clandestine radio transceiver was. Its discovery spelled the end for Jean-Paul Cuvillier. Torture commenced on the spot: the exact location of the English agent was demanded. The NCO of the SS was sent posthaste to alert the German command that the Englishman might be found in the docks, taking advantage of the attack in progress. The torture was vicious, involving cigarette burns on the private parts, the insertion of burning matches beneath the toe- and fingernails and then the water treatment that left the old man gasping like someone drowning. Then the whip on the bared back, Cuvillier being roped down to his own bed.

The Frenchman refused to speak. Other and even cruder measures were taken but still there was no utterance. It was some while before the Gestapo man realized that Cuvillier was dead.

v

Aboard the *Castile*, lifeless and broken, Chief ERA Hollyman and his engine-room artificers had remained to await the final order to abandon. They had never been trained for use in a landing party, unlike stokers who underwent as much parade-ground activity as the seamen ratings, and were also instructed in the use of rifles and bayonets. Besides, Hollyman had a personal desire: to wreck the engine-room, assisted by his tiffies. No orders to this effect had come from the skipper but Hollyman was determined he wasn't going to leave any of his engine-room intact for any possible, even if unlikely, Nazi use.

Hollyman loved his engines: they were alive to him, things of shining beauty that made the ship go. Without the engines, the upper deck personnel would be useless. Hollyman had served a full two-year commission in the old *Castile* that last time, years ago now. He'd then been an ERA Third Class, ranking as a very junior petty officer. The engineer officer had been one of the old school, an ex-lower deck man, a basic ERA like Hollyman himself. Those being the days before the navy had brought in the bracketed letters to indicate an officer's branch, the engineer officer had had the rank of engineer commander. Engineer Commander Agar: Hollyman remembered him well. A taciturn man except when speaking of his engines. Hollyman remembered, as he went into the air-lock, now disjointed, distorted and useless from the impact and the exploding charges in the bows, a day in Pompey when old Agar had brought a party of boys aboard by permission of the Captain, school friends of his son from St Helens' College in Southsea. Agar had led them round the upper deck, the bridge, the flag deck and so on, indicating this and that monosyllabically and without much enthusiasm.

Then he had taken them down to the engine-room. There, he had been eloquent, almost poetic. He had aroused youthful interest, had communicated his own feelings well, and they had responded with eager questions. It had been a great day for Hollyman, detailed by his Chief ERA to attend upon the Engineer Commander. Agar had seen, Hollyman believed for the first time since the ship had commissioned, the young ERA's own enthusiasm; and thereafter had taken him as it were under his wing and taught him a lot, not least the vital importance of engine-rooms and engineers.

153

And now Hollyman was all set to smash up the very engine-room that old Agar had taken so much pride in. Never in his wildest dreams had Hollyman ever thought he would see the day when he did that. But it was better than having Nazis mucking about in it if the ship didn't flood, which she probably wouldn't, not right down anyway. The water was not deep where the *Castile* rested in her grave.

'All right, lads,' Hollyman said, taking a grip on the sledgehammer that he'd equipped himself with. The others had smaller hammers that would smash dials and gauges easily enough. 'Don't go and fracture any steam pipes, mind. We don't want to scald ourselves.'

He led the way down the ladders, fetching up on the starting platform where he gave the first swing of the sledgehammer, smashing the telegraph repeater from the wheelhouse. There were tears in his eyes but each swipe was, in his mind, a blow against a Nazi, a blow against Hitler in person. As the destruction in the engine-room went on, Yeoman of Signals Robbins, still on the flag deck, looked up at the NUC balls hoisted to the starboard yardarm on the mainmast, the foretopmast having gone when the director had been hit early on. Not Under Command . . . so much was obvious, considering the state of the ship, without the need for the signal but Robbins was a man of routine and punctiliousness and although Cameron had given no order about hoisting the NUC balls, spheres of tar-blackened canvas, that had been the first thing Robbins had done just before the *Castile* had hit the stone of the jetty.

Robbins grabbed for the guardrail as the ship gave a lurch. Settling a little farther as water entered, Robbins fancied. She was a sorry sight but she'd done her work. Robbins thought it was high time they all buggered off to the *Dionysus*. He looked at his watch and had a big surprise: they seemed to have hung about for hours but it was only a matter of ten minutes. There was now no sign of the commandos or of the naval landing parties but there was still plenty of noise and more fires had been started by the gunfire from the destroyer, fires concentrated in the dock area. Never mind the blockship business, Robbins thought, a good number of the big MTBs themselves had likely gone up by now.

vi

Ashore, the casualties had been heavy. Something like half the commandos were dead or wounded, together with a number of seamen and stokers, but the rest were fighting through towards the warehouse down by the railway tracks to the French capital. Chief Stoker Rump had done what he had predicted to himself: died. He had taken a stream of tracer across his throat and his head was virtually off. Alongside him Lieutenant(E) Rogers, who had accompanied the engine-room section of the landing parties, also died from the same burst. A number of women were going to miss his banter and his sex appeal and his generosity. As were his parents, unsuspectingly asleep in Outram Road, Southsea, not all that far across the water. Just the one son and in a day or two they would get the telegram from the Admiralty, the telegram that would bring their world to an end, like so many others.

Chief ERA Hollyman had no parents living but he had a wife and three children, now on the brink of adulthood and about to join the Andrew themselves, two as engine-room apprentices and one, the girl, as a Wren. Now they would have to journey on without him. As Robbins staggered a little to the *Castile*'s post-death lurch, so did Hollyman, who happened to be at the head of the steel ladder just below the platform giving access to the air-lock. He lost his balance and fell, and his sledgehammer fell with him. Hollyman went down head first and his head impacted on a jag of metal left by the hammers, and he died instantly in a welter of blood. The heavy sledgehammer fell with a lot of velocity behind it onto a steam pipe and did what Hollyman had wanted to avoid: it fractured the pipe and within seconds the engine-room was filled with scalding steam that seared Hollyman's body and stripped away the flesh.

13

THE FRENCH Resistance men with the Englishman felt reasonably secure in the Nazi uniforms: they had the look of warehouse guards, and no-one queried them. There was by this time total confusion in the port, and this was helping them. It also assisted the approach of the French girl, Marie, taking a big risk in crossing the railway tracks to come up in the lee of the warehouse where the men waited. At first she was unrecognized: the shaven head was covered now with a German steel helmet and her body was enclosed in a long cloak not unlike that of a Uhlan, the crack lancers of the German Army. In the red light of the burning buildings her face looked demoniac, the absence of hair giving her a convincingly male appearance.

It was the Englishman, the man referred to in London as Frank, who recognized her first, and incredulously. 'Marie! For God's sake, what – '

She stopped him. 'I bring news that must reach London,' she said breathlessly.

'The transmitter, Marie – '

'No, that is *kaput*. To contact other cells will take time, the Bosch is on the alert now. Jean-Paul's cafe . . . it has been watched by others as well as by the Gestapo, and I was given word that it has been raided and that Jean-Paul is dead. London must know of this.'

The Englishman took a deep breath. 'You'll not be safe here, Marie. You must come with us now, no going back.'

'Yes,' she said, and smiled. 'I was hoping . . . with all my heart I wish to go to England.'

ii

Now the combined British parties were closing in, advancing though slowly. Sub-Lieutenant Calcott, in the lead of his party of seamen, came up on the right of the commandos; over to the left John Brown was also drawing level, his face grim, streaming sweat, and filthy from the smoke. Brown felt surprise that anyone was still alive; but something had gone wrong for the German defence – it must have done. No reserves appeared to be coming in, the Nazis were seemingly already stretched to their limit. Brown recalled what Cameron had told him: the red herrings had been laid via the Resistance, and too many troops had been shifted out of the Dieppe area for the German comfort. That could be the only explanation. Suddenly, at the expected signal, the two flashes, came from ahead, Brown began to feel they were going to get away with it.

This far anyway. There would still be the long fight back towards the waiting destroyer, herself in danger. On leaving the *Castile* Brown had seen a red glow on the ship's fo'c'sle, evidence perhaps of a hit on one of the for'ard guns. It was touch and go, no safe forecasts. Brown was scarcely aware that he himself had been hit. Nothing much, a flesh wound in his left upper arm, but he felt the blood running down to his hand to drip onto the cobbles as he pressed on, firing more or less blind towards a blur of German troops.

At Brown's side Chief PO Barker, too old really for this sort of thing, moved doggedly on, sweating like the First Lieutenant, glad he hadn't been a pongo, spending peace and war on field manoeuvres and such. You could keep clean aboard a ship, there was a galley to produce hot food,

158

and your hammock was always there except when on watch or closed up at action stations. Barker thought of the wheelhouse, his own kingdom as chief QM. He wouldn't be seeing that again: the old *Castile* had had it now, just a hulk, a pile of metal without a heart, without motion, never again to lift to the scene of deep water, no more Eastern sunsets, no more flag-showing around the Empire, no more peacetime regattas in the Mediterranean. Once, during his last commission aboard the *Castile*, there had been an evolution, as the peacetime navy had called a suddenly ordered exercise, when the Home and Mediterranean Fleets had been together in Gibraltar for the annual combined manoeuvres. The Home Fleet had been under the overall command of Admiral Sir John Kelly; and he had on a sudden whim, for he was that kind of man, unpredictable and irascible, ordered an evolution which was to consist of the calling away of a steam picquet-boat from one of the battleships with the Royal Marine band embarked. They were to come alongside the Flag with the band playing a popular tune; and they approached the flagship to the strains of 'Has Anyone Here Seen Kelly. . . .' There was a lot of fun to be had in the pre-war navy; and Kelly himself had appreciated the initiative of the Royal Marines.

All in the past now: Barker had a strong feeling that the *Castile* of happy memory was to be his life's last ship. Well, it couldn't be a better one. He moved on, keeping his body bent, in the direction of the German defences.

Within the next half minute the vanguard of the combined landing parties had reached the lee of the warehouse, Brown and the commando major making it together.

iii

The BBC News services were still silent as to current events across the Channel as the families breakfasted later that morning; the newspapers, naturally, carried nothing either. In England it was mostly a fine day, even still in the West Country, where Mary Anne Blake scraped at the butter dish to find enough to cover at any rate one bite of the off-white wartime bread. Not that she was hungry, but mum was keeping an eye on her and looked worried, saying she must eat or she'd be ill.

'I'm not hungry, Mum, I'm not really.'

'That's not the point, dear. Your body needs its nourishment.'

Mary Anne sighed and ate. Not that there was much to eat: an egg a week, tiny rations of butter, fats, meat eked out with fish – one of Peter Blake's colleagues in the estate agents, a man with a disability that kept him from the call-up, did the odd bit of fishing and he brought some round from time to time, rather to Mrs Larkspur's disquiet: although she was grateful for the fish she suspected that Mr Torrence had an eye for a young grass widow and although she didn't like her son-in-law she did feel she should be watching his interests to that extent. But she didn't actually say anything; you couldn't really, considering the fish.

'What are you going to do this morning, dear?' she asked.

Mary Anne shrugged. 'What is there to do?'

'Well, I don't know, dear.' Mrs Larkspur brightened for a moment. 'Mrs Perrin could do with a hand. National Savings.' Each community had its National Savings campaign, for saving was patriotic and helped the war effort. 'And next week's War Weapons Week in Bodmin, remember. I dare say Peter would like to think you were helping with that . . . helping to keep Britain armed, you see, dear. Him and his ship and all.'

Some two hundred miles east of Bodmin Evelyn Brown took a hasty breakfast consisting of a cup of strong coffee and a succession of nervously-puffed cigarettes. With the coffee she also took two aspirins: she felt off-colour, not just a hangover. It could scarcely be the start of morning

160

sickness or anything like that connected with the life said to be stirring within her. Whose life? Would she ever really know the answer to that?

Would John believe that it was his, even if it was? Or had he genuinely no idea in the world of how she spent her time when he was away?

She believed he had not. A simple soul, a seaman, who believed what he was told, not being himself a liar. Which, she knew, was what she was. Nothing like facing up to oneself, she thought, staring across the kitchen table towards a mirror in the hall, visible through the open door. The face stared back at her, hollow-eyed, rather gaunt, otherwise pretty. She had nice hair: John had said so, often. So had other men. She couldn't help it if she was over-sexed, plenty of women were, as well as men. Sex wasn't a matter of *which* sex . . . she went back to facing up to herself, seeing herself as one day God, if he existed, would judge her. Facing up to herself, she confessed to God at the same time in effect. You couldn't ever fool God, so why try to fool yourself, why *not* be honest? She believed God would understand in any case. He wasn't an earthly judge, or a prison warder, or a policeman, or some dreadful moralizing do-gooder in a flat hat and tweed coat and skirt. He would understand what she missed; it was a natural act. Other men were just surrogates for an absent husband, nothing more than that.

Or was that, before God and herself, honest?

Not entirely. She stubbed out her cigarette, lit another. John was a good man but she found him dull. Dull, dull, dull. No imagination, dedicated to the Service. So was her father but with a difference. And her father had never been dull; there had always been a flirtation going on somewhere. She couldn't see John having a flirtation; many wives would have been glad enough of that, of course. So should she be – and probably was. She'd never been put to the test.

Another cup of coffee, another cigarette and she left the

161

flat and walked along the High Street to catch the bus into Portsmouth. There had been an air raid during the night but she hadn't been aware through a gin sleep, and was surprised, coming in on the bus, to find fresh damage, and smoke that reached out towards Cosham from North End. The fire engines were still at it. It had been largely incendiaries but with some high explosive as well. One of the roads that had been hit badly had been the one where Yeoman of Signals Robbins' sister-in-law, so recently widowed, lived. She and the boys: all three were somewhere beneath the rubble. Bad news once again for Robbins if ever he lived to hear it.

The civilians were in it just as much as the armed forces.

That thought came to Bess Marty at about the same time as Evelyn Brown looked out at the fire appliances and the rescue services in Portsmouth. Skegness was having its troubles as well. There was a vast explosion that sent Bess Marty to the window of the lodgings. Down below, the landlady rushed into the street. People were everywhere. It wasn't an air raid, there were no aircraft to be seen, but there was smoke and flame some way off.

The landlady spoke to some of the people and after a while a policeman was seen coming along on a bicycle. After a word with him the landlady called up to Bess.

'One of ours, Mrs Marty, a bomber, damaged over the sea.'

The story emerged later: the pilot had been seen to be doing his best to avoid the town but a wing had dropped off and he'd come down on the outskirts, dropped like a stone onto some bungalows. There had been a lot of people killed, a lot seriously injured.

That brought things very close to Bess Marty. The things that happened . . . too late, had she but known it, she got down on her knees and prayed for Arthur's safety. Send him back to me, she asked from the bottom of her heart, send him back safe.

iv

There was a hit aft, surprisingly: there was little of the

Castile left to give offence, to attract gunfire, but there it was, a shell that took one of the silent after ack-ack guns, put out of action earlier, and ripped it from its mounting.

Batten said, 'They've brought up artillery, sir.'

'Seems like it. Look, Pilot. You're doing no good here, we'll not move again! Get below and swim for it, across to the *Dionysus*.'

'What about you?'

'I stay, Pilot. I stay till the landing parties get back.'

'I'll stay with you, sir.'

'Don't be a bloody fool, Pilot.'

'I'd rather stay,' Batten said. His voice was flat, wanted no argument. Cameron thought what the hell. He started to ask why then cut himself off in time. He knew why: Batten didn't want, when on leave, to be drawn back to a pile of rubble in Liverpool and be faced with thoughts of what might have been if a certain Nazi aircraft hadn't dropped a certain bomb at a certain time. Often enough people decided they didn't want to live. Cameron thought about his mother, now a widow. She and his father had been exceptionally close and for a long time now his father had been shorebound, home every night. There must be a terrible void. It was the same for countless numbers of widows but this was his mother he was concerned with, and on account of the exigencies of the service, the exigencies of war, he had been unable to be any comfort to her. And the future? The future could go three ways: either he would be killed, or he would be taken prisoner, or he would come through and sail back to UK aboard the *Dionysus*. One chance in three that he might, somewhat late, be for a while at his mother's side. . . .

'I'd rather stay,' Hugh Batten said again.

'All right, Pilot – and thank you.' Cameron reached out and clasped the navigator's shoulder briefly. He was glad enough of the company as the long, slow minutes ticked past and the shore fighting continued in smoke and fire and sound. The German gunners fired again, but this time towards the waiting destroyer: Cameron believed that the shell that had hit the *Castile* had in fact been intended for the *Dionysus*, which was firing back with rapid salvoes, presumably taking the gun-flashes as the point of aim. Cameron and Batten ducked as there came a whistle overhead: another shell, passing across the bridge. It missed the *Dionysus* and there was an explosion on the opposite shore.

'Self-inflicted wound,' Cameron said with a grin.

There was no response from Batten. He was living a scene that in fact he had never been witness to, since he'd been at sea when his family and home had gone up beneath the Nazi bombs, but it would have been something like this, the fires of hell, the sounds of fury. The pressing of a button somewhere in the war-torn sky, the opening of bomb doors in the belly of an aircraft, the clusters of egg-like death-canisters falling, the blotting out of human lives and the wreckage of the lives that had been left behind. So many well-meaning people had said to Hugh Batten that he would get over it, given time: time, they said, was the great healer.

He didn't believe it.

And he didn't really want to get over it, either. He felt that in a sense that would be a betrayal. They had an answer to that, too: he needn't ever forget. That was a different thing from getting over it. Life had to go on.

All the clichés. They simply didn't help. The wound was as raw now as ever it had been. Nevertheless Batten had a religious belief. He believed they would meet again. It couldn't be too soon for him.

Standing there on the bridge of the *Castile* the war sounds began to fade. He was thinking back into the past, his mind going as it were astern until it came into the happy, tranquil days before the outbreak of war. He'd been second officer in the *Empress of Scotland* when he'd got engaged to Valerie, a passenger from Montreal to Liverpool, a young girl returning home after spending a few months with

Canadian relatives. It hadn't been just a sea romance: Batten had kept in touch after Valerie had disembarked, had been to her home, taken her to meet his parents. Two more voyages later he'd had long leave and they'd become engaged, and married six months after, quite a big wedding at the country church in the village where her parents lived, a quiet little place near Chester. Then back to sea, missing her but with the comforting thought of a wife to go back to. *Just a wee wifie waiting. . . .* That refrain had often run through his mind during the long night watches out across the North Atlantic and home again to Liverpool. They'd bought the small house on a mortgage soon after the wedding and they had been ideally happy, though Batten had found the sea life had a different aspect. A man wanted to be with his wife; and he had started to think seriously about trying to find a job ashore, no easy matter for a seafarer, all of whose qualifications were of the sea. Master Mariners' certificates of competency rang few bells away from salt water. There was the Trinity House Pilotage, there were harbour masters' berths, there were berths as instructors in the training ships, and that was about the lot. Hugh Batten, in early 1939, had struck lucky: he was accepted as chief instructor in seamanship with second officer's rank aboard the training ship *Conway*, an old ship of the line, under square sail, now long past seagoing. He was to take up his appointment in October.

On 3 September Neville Chamberlain had made his broadcast: 'This country is now at war with Germany.' That was that: Batten had volunteered for the Royal Naval Reserve, to go to sea in the warships. The younger men were needed at sea; the old hands could do the training jobs.

'Pilot.'

Batten came back to the present, and turned towards Cameron. Cameron said, 'Miles away. I've spoken to you three times.'

'I'm sorry,' Batten said.

'I'm not criticizing. I told you, you needn't be here.'

'I said – '

'Yes, I know. And I think I understand. I – just wondered if you wanted to talk.' Cameron paused. 'We may not have much time left.'

'No.'

'Well? We both have our losses, Pilot. I've not said anything about this until now, but just before we left Scapa I had word that my father had died. I'm not suggesting that's to be compared with – what you've suffered. But it helps to talk, I believe. For both of us, perhaps.'

Batten said, 'I'm very sorry, sir. About your father. Didn't he – '

'He served aboard this ship – yes. Lieutenant RNR, doing your job. A quarter of a century ago. That makes the *Castile* very personal to me. Now more than ever. It's my – ' Cameron broke off as a shout came from the yeoman of signals. 'What was that, Robbins?'

'Landing parties, sir! Coming back, I reckon, sir.'

14

THEY WERE COMING back as if out of the very jaws of hell, a straggle of survivors with what looked like Nazi troops in the middle. In the light of the fires Cameron saw the ragged camouflage battle-dress of the commandos, blood-soaked in too many cases. Bullets flew, tracer that could easily be seen arcing from the Nazi advance behind the landing parties. Hugh Batten beat Cameron to the Oerlikon in the starboard bridge wing. There was a prolonged stutter from the Oerlikon and some of the Germans fell, the rest slowed, and then fire was opened on what was left of the *Castile*. Batten fired blind, head down beneath the cover of his steel helmet, and more Germans fell. He used up all the available ammunition. Bullets swept across the bridge from the shore and Cameron felt a stinging sensation in the fleshy part of his right upper arm, just below the shoulder, and another nick on his head.

The commandos with the seamen and stokers closed the gap. Aft on the quarterdeck, the engine-room artificers saw that the survivors were going to come aboard rather than try to swim direct for the destroyer. They stood by to lend a hand. Wounded men were not going to be able to jump across the gap between ship and caisson. There was no sign of the commando major: Brown appeared through the whorls of smoke, demoniac, acting as rearguard along with

Ordinary Seaman MacTavish, firing back towards the German troops as their charges made as fast as possible for the *Castile*. Many of them carried wounded men. One of the first to leap across from ship to shore was the surgeon lieutenant. He was caught in mid leap by a stream of tracer, and fell into the murky water between. A moment later another shell took the *Castile* amidships. Metal fragments flew and the searchlight platform disintegrated along with one of the multiple pompoms, its barrels already twisted out of shape in the earlier exchange of fire.

From the bridge Cameron saw Brown stumble and fall; and then saw MacTavish bend to help him up. So far as could be seen, Sub-Lieutenant Calcott was the only officer remaining, and a little in front of him was Chief PO Barker.

ii

It was a very far cry from the counter at the bank. The Nazis were a different kettle of fish from Calcott's manager. For the first time in his young life Calcott was seeing and feeling sheer hate, murderous hate. It was them or him. He had little thought in his head for the seamen or the commandos or the men of the French Resistance or the man they had come to bring off to safety in the UK: he fought for himself. He fired his revolver blind into the German pursuit, running backwards until he tripped and fell flat, hurting his back on a bollard as he went. He screamed; no-one seemed to hear. He rolled over and tried to get up, but found he couldn't.

Then he saw the chief gunner's mate running back towards him.

Bullshit Shine said, 'You're not dead yet.' He bent and slid his hands beneath the sub's shoulders and hoisted him to his feet. 'Can you walk, sir?' he asked, breathlessly.

'No, I –'

'Hold tight, then.' The chief gunner's mate lifted Calcott and laid him across his shoulder. Calcott dangled like a doll. Shine moved for the ship, fast as he could. The job was done: they had the British agent. Now all they had to do was to retain him and get him across to the *Dionysus*, and then get out.

Bullshit Shine thought: some hope! Some hope for all of us, he thought. It was all crazy, something thought up by the bloody barrack stanchions safe ashore in the Admiralty and the Special Operations Executive, the boyos that sent other men to do their dirty work for them. Bullshit Shine thought agents, or spies to give them their proper name, were very dirty. But of course they had their uses, that he couldn't deny. And this one had to be got out of France come what may, out of German hands.

And bugger Mr Calcott. Shine didn't believe he was badly hurt, just winded more like. Shine had seen him go down and since he hadn't got up again he'd run back. Now Mr Calcott looked like being the means of depriving Rosie of a husband, someone who wouldn't ever again be getting off the Pompey train and nipping into the Fountain for a pint before going on home up Redhill Road. A moment later Shine's burden gave a curious sort of lurch and all of a sudden the weight became a dead weight as life departed. Shine felt the surge of blood and something else run down over his shoulder. He moved into the lee of a warehouse and gently laid the body down. The head had been disintegrated by a bullet and was oozing: no use carrying him on. Shine turned and fired at a squad of Nazis moving past the end of the warehouse, then moved himself. Rosie might have a chance yet of avoiding a widow's pension. Coming up to the *Castile*'s shattered side he saw a number of what looked like uniformed Nazis being assisted aboard: the Resistance party, though this Shine didn't know, with the escaping British agent. One of the persons appeared to be a girl: some clothing had come adrift and men didn't have breasts. In the fires' light Bullshit Shine saw that she was potentially good-looking; he wondered about her, fleetingly, then reflected that the Frenchies had plenty of

women in the ranks of the Resistance which was what she
must be. He stopped wondering when he saw Lieutenant
Brown lose his footing and drop down into the water
between ship and shore, like the doctor had done. He saw
something else: Ordinary Seaman MacTavish, also going
over, but voluntarily.

Safer down there?

Not really. Bullshit Shine shook his head in wonder. You
never knew a man's worth until there was a crisis.

iii

'Yeoman!'

'Yessir?'

'Is your Aldis working?'

'Yessir. Battery set, sir.' All the ship's electric power had
gone off the board some while earlier.

'Make to *Dionysus*, lay alongside fast as you can.'

'Aye, aye, sir.'

Robbins aimed his lamp and made the destroyer's call
sign. There was an immediate acknowledgement: Robbins
lost no time in passing Cameron's message. The destroyer
was on the move within the next half-minute, her screws
churning up the foul harbour water and raising the stench of
any French port, oil fuel and rotten fish and almost
non-existent sewage systems. The *Dionysus* came in close,
ripping out davits, crunching her side along that of the dead
Castile. Paintwork didn't matter now: just speed in
execution, to be followed by a panic embarkation and a
dash away from the German guns, a running of the gauntlet
out of Dieppe – if they were lucky.

'Pilot –'

'Sir?'

'Stand by to abandon. Robbins, get down to the upper
deck, get across to the *Dionysus* fast as you can.'

'Aye, aye, sir.'

'You, too, Pilot. No point in –'

170

'I'm staying, sir.'

'Not this time, Pilot. Don't be a fool.'

Batten was stubborn. 'I'd rather –'

'An order, Pilot. You can still be of use in this bloody war. You have a duty. Don't duck it.'

Batten seemed still inclined to argue but evidently thought better of it. He turned away, saluted formally, his face grimly set in the demoniac red light of the fires along the jetty, the burning warehouses, the flashes of the guns. Alongside, the *Dionysus* was keeping up a continuous fire, the overall glow turning the white anti-flash gear of her guns' crews to a dull red. Batten started down the ladder. The yeoman of signals went for one last touch of the guardrail where he had carved his wife's name, caressed it with tears starting to run down his face. The old *Castile* . . . he was parting once again from his wife as well as from the old ship, that was how he felt about it, and it was one of the worst and bleakest moments of his life. Like the navigator he wouldn't have minded dying with the ship. But that was kind of defeatist really, and there might yet be a future. There was the wife's sister and who knew what might transpire? Clutching his Aldis lamp and its battery on a long lead, he followed Lieutenant Batten down the ladder to the upper deck, looking up and back just once as he went.

Cameron remained alone on the bridge. As Captain, his duty was clear. Everyone had to be got across first, then his turn would come. In the meantime there was nothing he could do. No ammunition left for the Oerlikon even. He folded his arms on the guardrail ahead of him and rested his head on them. In his mind's eye he saw his father, standing in the very same spot that Hugh Batten had been standing in, behind the binnacle. A curious feeling overcame him, a feeling that there was positively an after life and that his father, that much older man as he had become, now dead, was in fact there in spirit and was emanating approval.

Too soon, though: the job was far from done yet even if

his, Cameron's, part in it was temporarily suspended. There was still room for error, time for everything to go wrong. As so often in war, luck still had its part to play.

iv

'MacTavish!'

'Aye.'

Bullshit Shine peered down. He could just make out MacTavish, supporting the First Lieutenant's head clear of the water, the scummy water that slopped about between ship and jetty. 'How is he, MacTavish?'

'He's hurt. Knocked his head.'

'But alive?'

'Oh, aye, he's alive yet.'

'Stand by for a line,' Shine called down. Then he jumped for the ship and felt a moment of immense relief that he was back aboard, whatever state the *Castile* was in. Barker jumped a little behind and Shine said he wanted a line to send down to fetch up Jimmy the One before he got himself crushed, which could happen if the ship surged. Barker got hold of a length of hemp, quickly fashioned a bowline at its end, and sent it snaking down towards where he could see the two men. MacTavish caught it and began fiddling about with it, inexpertly. Barker shouted down.

'Call yourself a seaman! Use the bowline, lad, get it under his arms.' Barker held the other end of the line, standing by to take the strain and heave the First Lieutenant up the ship's side to safety. Safety of a sort, anyway. Down below MacTavish continued fiddling about and oaths came up: the working space was, to say the least, restricted and the water was cold, which didn't help cackhanded fingers. MacTavish wondered why he'd gone down; he had no love for officers, they'd not done anything for him, ever, in his view. But it had been an almost reflex action: Jimmy the One was British, some sort of feeling had penetrated of all belonging to the same ship, and

172

MacTavish nourished his hatred of Nazis. That was about it.

He fumbled and succeeded despite blasphemies from Barker. The rope went beneath the First Lieutenant's arms and MacTavish yelled up towards the sky.

'All right, you can stop your blethering, he's fixed.'

'At last, eh. Ready to hoist, MacTavish?'

'Aye, hoist away.'

With two able seamen Barker took up the slack of the rope and then took the strain as Brown's weight came on. Within a minute the First Lieutenant was brought over the side and laid on the deck. His face was white and there was a big lump already beginning to show on his forehead, just at the hair line, but he was stirring and opening his eyes. 'He'll be all right, I reckon,' Barker said. 'Did I hear the order from the bridge, to abandon?'

'You did,' Bullshit Shine said.

'Best get across, then. Where's those Frenchies?'

The Frenchies were already aboard the *Dionysus*: they wouldn't be seeing France again until after the war was won. With them was Frank and the girl, the Comtesse de Perpignan. All around the noise continued: the destroyer was pumping out shells, firing across the decks of the *Castile*. Men were jumping the guardrails all along the upper deck, crowding aboard the *Dionysus*. It was not yet dawn: the whole operation had taken little more than half an hour. Ordinary Seaman Quentin, looking at his watch, was disbelieving, and checked the time with Stripey Bottomley once they were both aboard the destroyer. Stripey was bleeding profusely from a gash on his forehead and blood was pouring down into his eyes. He didn't see who was speaking. He answered, 'Can't see me watch, sir.'

An apparent officer's voice . . . Quentin didn't disillusion him, not wishing to embarrass. At least he had that qualification for commissioned rank – he spoke with the right accent. He wasn't too sure that he had any of the others, the attributes that made up what the navy called

OLQ – Officer-Like Qualities. He knew he hadn't been all that forward in action, though at least he hadn't run away. He didn't feel like a leader, wouldn't have known what to do had he been left in charge as an officer. You followed orders, of course, obeyed the last order if the leader was killed, but then there came the time when you had to think and initiate and lead, since you couldn't go on for ever on a dead man's word. But he had a feeling he was going to get that commission. Just the fact that he'd been a part of the *Castile*'s mission, the fact of having been in very intense action, would go a long way with the selection board when he got back to the depot to face the captains and the rear-admirals who would compose the board. Or it might not.

They would ask him: what was it like, my boy?

Bloody awful, sir.

Incipient hysteria? There would be coughs, exchanged glances. But he would go on.

Bloody murder, sir. Bloody murder. I felt like throwing up. I felt like running away but I was more afraid of that really. It's hard to see what war's all about. The way some of us died, guts torn out, entrails on the ground, raw, gaping throats, smashed heads, charred bodies. . . .

Yes, well, that's enough, Quentin.

Yes, sir. I'm sorry, sir.

You've had a rough time, of course. Perhaps the medical officer should be asked to report.

Psychologist, more like.

'You there – Quentin!'

Quentin turned, startled. Bullshit Shine faced him, square and hard. 'Stop that bloody blubbering. In for a commission – aren't you, lad?'

'I – I'm not so sure, Chief.'

'You'll make it. You didn't do so bad, all things considered. Don't give up. Now come with me. And you, MacTavish.'

'Where to?'

174

'Back to the *Castile*, that's where. The bridge . . . I just see the Captain. Just before 'e slid on 'is backside like.'

'Hit, Chief?'

'I don't know, do I?' Shine was already clambering over the guardrail. 'Going to find out. Smack it about, now, the two o' you.'

As they went, there was a shout from the bridge of the destroyer: her Captain wanted to be away. It was Chief Petty Officer Shine who shouted back. It wouldn't take long, he said. They wouldn't leave without Lieutenant-Commander Cameron. Two minutes, the destroyer captain called down. Two minutes flat, and then he was putting his engines astern to come off and away.

Followed by the two ordinary seamen, Shine moved fast, half slithering along the deck because of the blood. Firing came from the shore: the destroyer's close-range weapons gave covering fire, holding the Nazis back, sending them running for cover behind a blazing warehouse.

Shine started up the first of the ladders to the bridge. He was way ahead of the two ordinary seamen. MacTavish was next behind, then Quentin. When Shine was half-way up the ladder something came adrift above his head. Quentin shouted a warning but it was too late for Shine. From its height in the port corner of the flag deck, the big signalling projector, the 32-inch, fell straight as a die. It landed fair and square on Bullshit Shine's head. It virtually drove both head and neck down into his torso. He fell and lay spreadeagled on the deck while the SP bounced away over the side. It was MacTavish who went forward and lifted off the steel helmet. With difficulty: the rubber lining-band had been driven down, over Shine's eyes. The steel itself had impacted hard against the skull, which was splintered and oozing brain matter. What was left of the head lolled sideways with a curious upward tilt that exposed the adam's apple. The neck was broken.

This time, Quentin did throw up. Shine's body, though it must already have been dead, had twitched and jerked for

175

perhaps three or four seconds. Brief as that terrible sight had been, Quentin knew he could never forget it.

15

QUENTIN'S STOMACH seemed to rise and fall, sickeningly even though now empty. Drily, he retched. He wanted nothing so much as to run, to run anywhere away from what lay on the deck in front of him.

He turned, faced aft, licked at his lips. MacTavish said, 'That'll do no good at all.'

'What won't?'

'I saw it in your face,' MacTavish said. 'If we run now, they'll get us. The officers will. Bloody court martial. We've got to get to the bridge. So they see us there – get it?'

'The Captain –'

'Maybe he's alive, maybe he's not. Come on now.' MacTavish's face streamed sweat: there was fear in his eyes, he was as afraid as Quentin. But discipline was exerting its ordained authority: he was as scared of the naval power as he was of the enemy. Quentin shook like a leaf. The firing had started again and tracer was arcing over the bridge high above. Then they heard footsteps on the ladder immediately below the bridge itself.

They both looked. 'It's the skipper,' MacTavish said. 'Coming down . . . we've been bloody heroes for sod all. . . .'

It had been a near thing and Cameron had been knocked out temporarily. Blood streamed down his face from a graze above his right eye where a bullet had slid past. There might be bone damage, he didn't know. He felt groggy, his legs reluctant to give him support when he pulled himself upright, clutching the voice-pipes that festooned the fore screen of the bridge.

He moved unsteadily for the ladder. With *Dionysus* alongside and waiting, this was the moment to go. His own decks were deserted now. Almost, anyway. As he came past the binnacle and, holding tight to the guardrail, took the treads of the ladder, he saw the two seamen below.

'Who's that?'

'MacTavish, sir.' Oh yes – MacTavish. There had been some trouble, something as yet unresolved. 'All right, MacTavish. I'm all right. Get across to *Dionysus*. That's –' Something happened to his legs. He crumpled, lay back against the guardrail, swinging from his hand-grip. Then things went blank and he slid down the ladder and lay in a heap at the bottom.

MacTavish swore. Then he climbed, told Quentin to stay on the lower ladder and take the skipper's feet when he lowered him, and guide him down. MacTavish lifted Cameron by the shoulders and dragged him towards the next downward ladder. When they reached the deck they took Cameron between them and, staggering and lurching, carried him aft to skirt the shattered searchlight platform and the after splinter screen, around to the port side and the hands waiting on the upper deck of the *Dionysus* to assist them across. There was no time now to think too much about Bullshit Shine: the fact of death had been all too obvious and the destroyer captain was impatient to be away. As Cameron was brought aboard the orders were already being passed: wheel amidships, engines half astern.

Dionysus slid away, coming round, once she was clear of the *Castile*, to head her bows for the turn in the centre of the channel after which she would move under full power for the harbour entrance and the passage outward through the arms of the breakwater. As she made that first turn her Captain took up a sound-powered telephone and spoke to his WT office.

'Make the transmission now.'

Within four minutes the urgent signal had been received in the Operations Rooms at the Admiralty in London; an officer of the WRNS, trim in dark blue coat and skirt with two light blue stripes on either cuff, approached the Duty Captain.

'Transmission from *Dionysus*, sir. Just her call sign.'

The Duty Captain nodded briefly, then took up a red-coloured telephone. The call was answered at once. The Duty Captain said, 'Transmission received, sir. That means she's fighting her way out now –'

'Mission successful?'

'I think we can read that into it so far, sir. Will you contact C-in-C Portsmouth?'

'No sooner said than done.' The call was cut; the Duty Captain sat back at full arms' stretch from his desk. All the arrangements had been made: wireless orders would go from C-in-C to a cruiser squadron steaming dangerously exposed in the English Channel well south of the port of Newhaven in Sussex, fast, heavily armed ships that would close towards the French coast and be handy when the *Dionysus* came through. The Duty Captain expected something of a battle: the Germans would be starting to react even though the overall time had been short, as short in fact as had been expected at the planning stage. Units of the German Navy would be on their way to intercept in an attempt to stop *Dionysus* in her tracks before she could reach a British port. The Duty Captain wondered about casualties. Already there must surely have been many of them. So many families to be informed, but that, thank

God, would not be his job. When would the news be released, assuming the mission had been in fact successful, that Hitler's latest sea threat had been aborted? Not yet, that was certain: the Admiralty was never very forthcoming. On the other hand, Winston always loved to announce good news. He just might decide to do it off his own bat, and in the House. As to the cutting-out of that agent, that would remain a secret until after the war was over, and maybe not made public even then. Intelligence was a minefield.

iii

Everything left in the port was firing. A good deal of the defensive capacity of Dieppe had been destroyed by the gunfire from the British ships, but it looked as though the Nazis had dragged in replacements, mostly medium artillery, Cameron believed. Still groggy, he had made it plain to the surgeon lieutenant aboard the *Dionysus* that he had no intention, at this final stage, of remaining below either in the sick bay or a cabin that could have been made available for him. He had been on the bridge coming in, he was going to be on the bridge, even someone else's, going out. And the Captain of the *Dionysus* had had no objections.

Not wishing to intrude in any way, Cameron huddled himself into an after corner. As the destroyer gathered speed outwards, he was joined by John Brown, also rather the worse for wear but mobile and preferring to be on deck.

'Casualties?' Cameron asked, dreading the answer.

'Heavy, sir. I haven't a full count – we'll have to muster by the open list soon as possible, of course – but my reckoning is fifty to sixty.'

'Particular names, Number One?' Good God, Cameron thought, they'd sailed with only eighty-plus. . . .

'The Chief GI –'

'Bullshit Shine gone?'

180

'I'm afraid so. Froggett. Blake. Calcott. Hollyman, the Chief ERA. Chief Stoker Rump. Others. . . .' Brown paused and when he went on his voice was bitter. 'So many of the old *Castiles*, the ones from earlier commissions. Old Marty earlier.'

'Yes. . . .'

'But I remain.'

Cameron looked at him in the light of the gunfire. 'What's that supposed to mean, Number One?'

Brown grinned mirthlessly. 'The bad penny turns up again. I have the feeling I'll not be all that welcome, back home.'

Cameron didn't say anything to that. It wasn't his business; and it was not hard to arrive at something of the truth. It was by no means unusual for those who went down to the sea in ships either in peace or war. Brown didn't say any more either; they stood there, feeling the wind of the destroyer's passage. Having come in, her navigator now had first-hand knowledge of the exit channel and enough confidence to leave the port at full speed. So the *Dionysus* was thundering for the breakwater at around thirty-two knots. Her speed was making it difficult for the shore gunners to lay on their target, and every turn of the screws took her closer to safety and the extended arms of the British cruiser squadron moving south. As she went, the destroyer's guns were in continuous action, spitting back at the enemy. As Cameron watched there was a big explosion on the shore as a battery was hit and went up. A brilliant flash of light filled with jags of rock and metal and with bodies whirling about, arms and legs extended, like rag dolls spilling out their innards, blood instead of sawdust.

Suddenly Brown said, 'D'you know something, sir?'

'What?'

'If I had my time over again . . . I'd be a bloody pacifist.'

'You, Number One?'

'Yes, me.' Brown gestured towards the still burning gun-battery. 'It's horrible. I'm not thinking of the bloody

181

Nazis, though I suppose they're human too. It's *our* people. Blokes like Shine, and Froggett, and Hollyman, and Marty. All good men, all with families. Same goes for the Germans too, of course. In some cases, that is.' Brown seemed to be rambling now. 'It's a bloody waste – isn't it?'

'Yes, it is. But they were all trained to it, Number One. All their adult lives, anyway until they were out on pension and thought they were done with it.'

'I was trained for it too,' Brown said. 'It doesn't make it any easier to watch.' Then he turned the subject. 'Nearly at the breakwater, sir. Nearly out. Nearly but not quite. They seem to be ready for us. Not that I find that surprising. See what I mean?' He pointed ahead. The arms of the breakwater were lined with heavy guns, big field pieces drawn into position by tracked vehicles. In the fore part of the bridge the destroyer captain spoke down the voice-pipe direct to his engine-room. Cameron could guess the message easily enough: more speed, any extra knot that could be squeezed out and never mind damage to bearings or whatever, just so long as those engines could carry her clear of the ranged guns.

A moment later the batteries opened, each gun in succession, right down the line to right and left. *Dionysus* fired still, the guns' crews sticking it to the end, fighting back almost in desperation now, keeping it up however little use their comparative pea-shooters might be against what had logically to be impossible odds. It was a question of time and it was a question of luck: They would be steaming slap into the guns until they made the exit, and then, if they got that far, they would have the guns behind them, firing still. Shells were everywhere, screaming overhead, bringing down masts and aerials – radar, WT. As had happened aboard the *Castile*, the director went, disintegrating into a shower of metal fragments from what had seemed like a direct hit. For'ard of the bridge Numbers One and Two guns disappeared in a cataclysm and fires started. With the conning-tower protected by its armoured

182

screen, the destroyer rushed on, maintaining her course for the exit as the German guns thundered and flamed, closer now, and closer yet. On the bridge the Captain and navigator were alive but streaming blood from superficial wounds. Both the lookouts had died when the director went, so had the yeoman of signals, and their bodies lay contorted on the deck.

As the destroyer reached the channel between the breakwaters the German fire was suspended: for the shore guns to fire now would be virtually for one breakwater's artillery to fire direct at the other. As the noise and gun-flashes wavered, Cameron saw a weird glow just behind the breakwater on the destroyer's port side.

iv

By Admiralty telegram the word went through, a couple of days later. Bess Marty opened the buff-coloured envelope with shaking fingers, knowing before she did so what it contained. She sat down very suddenly as she read. She didn't say a word. The landlady, who had also suspected when the telegram boy had come, made cups of tea and sat with her in silence, not knowing what to say, knowing she could offer no comfort, sensing that speech would not be welcome. It was a long while before Bess Marty did speak, then she said, 'Well, that's that. All those years. All over now. He was a good man, was my Arthur.'

Rosie Shine was out when her telegram arrived, walking the dog as she was used to do, and as she had done a couple of days earlier she met old Hartley, who lifted his hat.

'Morning, Mrs Shine.'

'Good morning, Captain Hartley.'

'Lovely day. . . .'

'Yes, isn't it?' Links Lane, up past Stallard the dairyman's, was fresh with dew, the sun coming up to dispel it gradually. The wartime postwoman was on her delivery round, bicycle-mounted. Rosie called out, 'Anything for me, is there?'

'No, Mrs Shine.'

'Still no news,' Captain Hartley remarked. 'Well –
Careless Talk Costs Lives, eh? Remember me to your
husband when you write, won't you?' Lifting his hat again,
the old mariner moved away and Rosie began calling the
dog. That cat again . . . she didn't get the news until, on
that bright, fresh morning, she went back up Redhill Road
and found the telegram boy waiting.

Mary-Anne Blake's telegram was brought to her by her
mother, whose knowing face was drawn with tension,
agonizing for her daughter.

'You open it, mum.'

'All right, dear.' In the doorway, Mr Larkspur hovered,
the *Daily Telegraph* drooping from his hand and his mouth
sagging in anticipation of a scene. Everybody knew what
telegrams meant in wartime.

'Read it,' Mary-Anne said in an unusually harsh voice.

'If you want me to, dear,' Mrs Larkspur said, and began
reading. 'Regret to inform you that your husband
Temporary Acting Lieutenant Peter Walmsley Blake Royal
Naval Volunteer Reserve has been reported . . .' Why ever
did they have to be so formal, spelling it out in full? Mrs
Larkspur choked a little when she saw Mary-Anne's face,
then read on since it seemed expected of her. 'Been
reported killed in action.'

Mary-Anne gave a high scream, very suddenly, but, like
Bess Marty, didn't cry. Not until Mrs Larkspur went to her
and held her tight. 'Oh, my poor little girlie, my poor little
girlie. . . .' Now she really was her mother's little girl
again: it was an ill wind, Mrs Larkspur thought. She had
never lost her maternal instinct and poor Peter Blake had
been something of an interruption if the truth be told.

Ordinary Seaman Quentin had been one of those who
had died aboard the *Dionysus* as the destroyer had fought
her way out of the port. His father received the telegram
without embellishments: later, when Cameron was able to
deal with the letters to the bereaved, he would know that

his son had gone beyond the call of duty, had been one of two men who had stayed behind aboard the *Castile* until they had rescued their Captain. In the meantime, one of the first things Quentin senior did was to telephone Cambridge, feeling his son's college ought to know. He'd met the boy's elderly tutor once, and thought he would like to talk to him now.

'I'm so sorry,' the old man said, his voice quavering a little with age. 'So very sorry . . . decent of you to let me know straight away, and personally. Your boy showed much promise, much promise. The war's a tragedy.' He had taken the call in the senior common room, where he was drinking a glass of dry sherry, La Ina, before his lunch. Ringing off, he spoke to an old crony. 'Young Quentin . . . don't *quite* remember him. Shadowy, don't you know. Though I do recall something. Navy rather than the more usual army . . . when he joined – yes. I said sailors were uncouth . . . or words to that effect. Philistines.' He gave a laugh as dry as the La Ina. 'No doubt he found that out for himself!'

It was one more sorrow for Yeoman Robbins' sister-in-law: Robbins had died aboard *Dionysus*, just before the destroyer had come clear of the port and the breakwater: a shell splinter had taken a slice off his head, not that she knew this. First her sister, then her husband, now the man she might have taken as a husband if he'd asked her, which she believed he would, given time. Now, as in Bess Marty's case, it was all over. Before it had ever begun. Her brother-in-law had been a good man, so delighted to get back into the Andrew as he'd called it, even more delighted to be drafted so short a time ago to the old *Castile* of happy memory. The ship hadn't done him much good in the end. The sister-in-law carried on with the washing-up, thinking of the dead man, so smart he'd been in his Number One uniform when he'd called round last, the double-breasted jacket, brass buttons, crossed flags and crown in gold on his right arm, crossed fouled-anchors and crown above the three Good Conduct chevrons, also in gold, on his left arm. By now, all that would be somewhere beneath the sea, she supposed.

Only one telegram was sent per family by a frugal Admiralty: Lieutenant(E) Rogers' parents were informed and Outram Road, Southsea, became a bleak place. Rogers' lady friends were not informed, or not all of them, since his parents had never known the half of it. They certainly didn't know about the possibly pregnant one and neither did the lady know their address: they could have been anywhere in the UK or out of it. So she was not informed. Her lover merely vanished and in course of time she would wonder why, bitterly, considering herself badly let down. She had never even met any of his friends: Rogers had been a prudent man, separating his girl friends out widely. The sea life gave one scope for that, and also experience.

When a telegram was delivered at the Fareham flat, Evelyn Brown was busy in the officers' club in Southsea. Her cleaning woman took the telegram and thought she ought to phone through, guessing like so many other recipients what it might well be. She asked if she should open it and read it.

'Yes, please,' Evelyn said, and caught her breath; at the same time catching her major's eye. He was often at a loose end and spent loose ends mostly in the club. 'Go on, Mrs Wotherspoon.'

It took Mrs Wotherspoon some while to open the envelope. She read slowly. 'Expect me about 1930 tonight stop have fourteen days leave.' There was a pause and heavy breathing. 'It's from your husband, Mrs Brown.'

'Yes, I see. Thank you, Mrs Wotherspoon. Goodbye.' Evelyn put down the phone. To the major she said, 'My husband. I thought –'

'He hasn't bought it, has he?'

'No. No, he's evidently very much alive and will be home tonight.'

186

The prognostications of the Duty Captain in the Operations Room had been correct: the Prime Minister, bucked by the success of a daring mission inspired by himself, made an announcement to a packed House of Commons: the Members were expectant because there had been a leak that something big was to be announced that afternoon.

The Prime Minister rose and broke a total silence.

'It is my pride and pleasure to announce a – ah – a splendid act of gallantry on the part of the British Fleet, an act of which the whole nation can be proud. A blow has been struck at the very heart of Herr Hitler's plans to savage our convoys . . . great damage has been inflicted on the port installations of Dieppe . . . the mission, despite I regret to say heavy casualties, has been wholly successful, the two ships involved having carried out their duty . . . the very heart of the port of Dieppe has been strangled, blocked. . . a blockship like the illustrious *Vindictive* at Zeebrugge . . . and the supporting destroyer, although severely damaged, making good her escape from the worst that the Narzis [sic] could do against her. We salute the memory of those who sacrificed their lives . . . and we honour those who came back through shot and shell to fight again another day.'

Cameron listened to the BBC News report of the Prime Minister's announcement from a bed in the Royal Naval Hospital at Haslar, where he had been transferred after *Dionysus* had entered the port of Newhaven in Sussex. He was to be kept under observation but the doctors had been reassuring that he would be fit for sea duty again within a couple of weeks. He had managed a quick telephone call to his mother in Aberdeen. As soon as the doctors let him go, he would come home, he said. There would be much for him to do, sad duties in connection with his father's estate and trawler fleet. But lying there in bed with plenty of time to think, his thoughts were chiefly of the *Castile* and all that had gone with her. His father's last wish: had he carried that out fully? He believed he had, to the best of his ability. But so many lives had gone, so many homes blasted. Inevitable in war, but. . . . There was always the but. Waste? If so, it was down to Hitler and his Nazi thugs.

There had been a final stroke of luck or none of them would have survived: that weird glow from just behind the breakwater that Cameron had seen as the *Dionysus* came abeam of the temporarily silent guns along the arms . . . he would possibly never be entirely certain, but it was likely that a shell from the destroyer's after guns, still in action, had landed fair and square on something like an ammunition dump, or an arsenal of some sort for the port's defence. What was quite certain was that the explosion when it came had been immense and literally shattering. It had taken out the shore guns on the destroyer's port side, obliterating them in a flash and their crews with them. Those on the starboard side had appeared shocked into total inaction until the *Dionysus* had passed at her high speed into clear water with the cruisers soon to close towards them. She had not entirely escaped the backlash: her upper deck was a shambles and more men had died, many of them the commandos. The survivors of the Royal Marines had acted as replacements for the naval guns' crews who had been killed at their action stations. Some of the French Resistance fighters had died also, coming foolishly on deck to yell Gallic defiance at the Nazis. The British agent, Frank, was safe below. So was the girl.

John Brown came to see Cameron, deviating on his way to Fareham.

'How's it going, sir?'

'Not too bad. Boredom's the worst thing in hospital, Number One. That, and regrets.' Cameron paused, his eyes holding a faraway look. 'Memories.'

'Yes, I know. Too bloody sharp and likely to remain so. It was murder, all the way through.' Brown gave him a quick look. 'There's a loose end. Sorry to bother you –'

188

'That's all right. What is it, Number One?'

Brown said, 'MacTavish. He came through.'

'Yes, I know. That charge.'

'Right.'

Cameron frowned. 'It still stands. It has to . . . he has to go through the rigmarole of Defaulters and Off Caps . . . even if only to have the charge formally dismissed. You know that, Number One. But after all that bloody business, all that action. . . .'

'Quite. He didn't hold back. Insubordinate and so on he may be, but he's no yellow-belly, nothing like that.' He paused. 'Of course, it's up to you, sir.'

'Well, Number One? You sound as though there's something else. Is there?'

'Yes, there is. The RPO was blown into little pieces, poor chap, and no-one bothered to salvage his charge sheets and police bumph. With all the casualties, there's just you and me left to know about it. So –'

'Forget it,' Cameron said. 'We just forget it, all right?'

'All right, sir.'

'Just a minute, though.' Cameron had thought of something. 'Batten – he came through. He was on the bridge when MacTavish was brought up.'

'That's taken care of, sir. Pending your decision I took the liberty of having a word with Batten. No worries there. Frankly, he didn't seem to be registering.'

'He has his own worries,' Cameron said. 'Got back safe, and no-one to go home to – poor old Pilot. In a sense, he survived for nothing. Still – that's so often the way of it in this war. The civilians –' He broke off. Everyone knew that in many ways the civilian population was getting the worst of the war. 'Now what about you, Number One? On your way home, I take it?'

'Home,' the First Lieutenant repeated in a curious tone. 'Yes, that's right. I'm going home. To Fareham. Home to the wife. I'm one of the lucky ones, aren't I?'

He turned away abruptly from Cameron's bedside and

189

strode towards the door, shoulders square. There was something purposeful about him. Cameron, who'd had those inklings earlier, felt that Brown was about to sort something out. He wished him luck.

190